Bolan was on the hunt, and that was all that mattered

He'd rest when it was finished, eat when there was time and bathe when he was sure that there was no more blood to spill.

This time, at least.

Because the hunt was never really over. Bolan's war was never done. There might be cease-fires, the occasional white flag of truce for mutual convenience, but he'd never sign a treaty with the predators who were his enemies. He couldn't fight them to a draw and walk away, believing that he'd managed to secure some short-term victory.

The war went on until he fell, or else became the last man standing on the battlefield. Right now, the battlefield was here, on Isla de Victoria. Tomorrow, if he lived, it would be somewhere else. New faces, varied motives, but the same old enemies.

War without end.

MACK BOLAN ®
The Executioner

#235 Plague Wind
#236 Vengeance Rising
#237 Hellfire Trigger
#238 Crimson Tide
#239 Hostile Proximity
#240 Devil's Guard
#241 Evil Reborn
#242 Doomsday Conspiracy
#243 Assault Reflex
#244 Judas Kill
#245 Virtual Destruction
#246 Blood of the Earth
#247 Black Dawn Rising
#248 Rolling Death
#249 Shadow Target
#250 Warning Shot
#251 Kill Radius
#252 Death Line
#253 Risk Factor
#254 Chill Effect
#255 War Bird
#256 Point of Impact
#257 Precision Play
#258 Target Lock
#259 Nightfire
#260 Dayhunt
#261 Dawnkill
#262 Trigger Point
#263 Skysniper
#264 Iron Fist
#265 Freedom Force
#266 Ultimate Price
#267 Invisible Invader
#268 Shattered Trust
#269 Shifting Shadows
#270 Judgment Day
#271 Cyberhunt
#272 Stealth Striker

#273 UForce
#274 Rogue Target
#275 Crossed Borders
#276 Leviathan
#277 Dirty Mission
#278 Triple Reverse
#279 Fire Wind
#280 Fear Rally
#281 Blood Stone
#282 Jungle Conflict
#283 Ring of Retaliation
#284 Devil's Army
#285 Final Strike
#286 Armageddon Exit
#287 Rogue Warrior
#288 Arctic Blast
#289 Vendetta Force
#290 Pursued
#291 Blood Trade
#292 Savage Game
#293 Death Merchants
#294 Scorpion Rising
#295 Hostile Alliance
#296 Nuclear Game
#297 Deadly Pursuit
#298 Final Play
#299 Dangerous Encounter
#300 Warrior's Requiem
#301 Blast Radius
#302 Shadow Search
#303 Sea of Terror
#304 Soviet Specter
#305 Point Position
#306 Mercy Mission
#307 Hard Pursuit
#308 Into the Fire
#309 Flames of Fury
#310 Killing Heat

The Executioner®
Don Pendleton's
KILLING HEAT

The ORGCRIME Trilogy

BOOK III

A GOLD EAGLE BOOK FROM
WORLDWIDE®

TORONTO • NEW YORK • LONDON
AMSTERDAM • PARIS • SYDNEY • HAMBURG
STOCKHOLM • ATHENS • TOKYO • MILAN
MADRID • WARSAW • BUDAPEST • AUCKLAND

First edition September 2004
ISBN 0-373-64310-1

Special thanks and acknowledgment to
Mike Newton for his contribution to this work.

KILLING HEAT

Nothing emboldens sin so much as mercy.
                                        —William Shakespeare
                                        Timon of Athens, III, v. 3

And if any mischief follow, then thou shalt give life for life, eye for eye, tooth for tooth, hand for hand, foot for foot, burning for burning, wound for wound, stripe for stripe.
                                        —*Exodus* 21: 23–25

I'm fresh out of mercy today and I'm dealing with the enemy in the only language he understands. From here on in, it's scorched earth all the way.
                                        —Johnny Bolan Gray

For Jessica Lynch and the other POWs
of the last Gulf War. Welcome home.

1

Cordillera Occidental, Colombia

"Tell me again," Keely Ross said, "why they build drug labs in the mountains."

"Closer to the coca trees," Johnny Gray replied. "You're wasting breath."

"Sorry," she told him, sounding not at all contrite.

He knew exactly how she felt. Frustration and fatigue combined to produce a sullen anger that could taint a soldier's judgment, throw him off his game unless he—or she—kept it under control.

It could be worse, he thought. Jack Grimaldi had been able to drop them two miles from the compound, so they didn't have to climb all the way from the lush river valley below. The air drop had put them closer to the action, saving them the best part of a day. But that just meant they were closer to the guns.

Closer to Mack, Johnny told himself, then wondered for the hundredth time if that was true.

Thirty-six hours had passed since Johnny Gray's brother was snatched by the enemy in Nassau. Even allowing for travel, that was still ample time for the enemy to work on

Mack, extract whatever secrets they deemed relevant and finish him. Or maybe they were keeping him alive just for the hell of it, seeing how many ways they could devise to make him scream.

Stop it!

The younger Bolan, known since age thirteen as Johnny Gray, focused on climbing, putting one foot in front of the other and watching out for traps along the way.

They were close now. He knew it from the map and aerial photos they'd studied—and he could smell it on the breeze. A glance at Ross told him she smelled it, too.

At the first stage of cocaine production, coca leaves were dumped into a tarp-lined pit and soaked in a mixture of water and gasoline. Barefoot peasants plodded back and forth through the lethal stew, helping break down the leaves into mulch. With the breeze in his face, Johnny smelled the gasoline fumes from a quarter mile away and knew they'd almost reached their goal.

There may have been a hundred coca compounds in the Cordillera Occidental mountains. Hell, for all he knew there could have been a thousand. But the one he smelled was different. According to the stories he'd picked up in Bogotá and Medellín, it wasn't just a cocaine lab. It was a prison, too.

It was the place where his brother was locked away.

Or maybe not.

Johnny recognized the danger going in. The odds were fifty-fifty, maybe higher, that he and Ross were walking into a trap. His informants could have been lying, despite their pain and fear of death—or maybe someone else had lied to *them*.

He wouldn't know until he crashed the party and had a look around. Ross had agreed with him, albeit grudgingly, and

Jack Grimaldi had supplied the wings—or rotors, in this case. With any luck, Grimaldi would pick them up again when they were done.

Assuming they were still alive.

Johnny and Ross were dressed in camouflage fatigues and bush hats, their hands and faces painted in contrasting shades of green and brown. They carried CAR-15 assault rifles. American equipment was seen so often in Colombia that there'd been no point in getting cute. Their side arms were Beretta autoloaders, and the combat knives on their belts were long enough to double as machetes if the forest got too thick. Spare magazines were belted to their waists and slung across their chests in bandoliers. Grenade pouches slapped heavily against their legs with every step.

Now all they needed was a target.

They slowed as they approached the camp. It was broad daylight, and the drug camps always had armed guards. If his brother was caged there, Johnny reckoned the security detachment would be doubled. There might even be a VIP or two on hand to grill him.

If it wasn't too late.

His brother might be past the point of needing any help, but there was still justice to be served.

Scorched earth.

Johnny had discussed that part of the plan with Ross and Grimaldi, and both of them agreed. If they couldn't help his brother, they could pay the bastards back.

Beginning now.

He stopped when they were close enough to hear the workers talking, and to smell a meal in preparation. Wood smoke and the scent of simple stew were competing with the reek of gasoline.

Ross whispered in his ear, "It looks like we're in time for lunch."

He turned and found her smiling at him through the war paint. Weary as she was from all they'd done in the past two weeks and their long hike through the woods, the lady still had spunk.

"Now that we're here," he said, "we may as well drop in."

Her smile brightened as she replied, "I thought you'd never ask."

ENRIQUE GARZA SIPPED his lukewarm beer and wondered why the damned refrigerator didn't function properly. Some said it was the altitude, others the ancient generator that kept light-bulbs winking on and off all night. Whatever, Garza didn't know why *he* should have to suffer for it, but El Jefe didn't ask his soldiers for opinions when he gave an order. Likewise, anyone who bitched and moaned about appointed tasks was not long for the world.

All things considered, Garza thought it could be worse. He had a relatively easy job—watching the peasants wade around in muck all day, keeping the chemists on their toes and out of mischief—and this week there might be some adventure, too.

Garza hadn't been sure if he should wish for some excitement on the job, or hope it never came. The trouble he'd been hearing of, in Panama and Nassau, was the sort that made him cringe, then hate himself for being soft.

No worries, he decided, swallowing another sip of beer. He'd deal with anything that happened. Why else had El Jefe given him so many men and guns?

He didn't really understand the plan, but that was fine. Garza was one who recognized his limitations and was pleased to work within them. He had fewer problems that way, and he seldom found himself outmatched.

The beer bottle was empty, and he rose to get another. Lukewarm *cerveza* was better than none, he'd decided, and the waiting had started to work on his nerves.

The sudden sound of a gunshot made him freeze. One hand was inside the small refrigerator, and he was leaning close to feel the cool air on his sweaty face. He waited for the shout that would explain how one of his lookouts had killed a snake, that there was nothing to it, no real trouble on the line.

But there was no all-clear.

Instead, after a moment that seemed to last hours, Garza heard half a dozen automatic weapons erupt in unison and someone shouting for help from the perimeter outside.

Was it the west side of the camp? He couldn't tell.

Garza released the beer bottle, not noticing that it bounced between his feet and rolled away. He left the door of the refrigerator standing open, snatched his automatic rifle—an Armalite AR-18 with folding stock—from the table where it lay and carried it outside.

Firing continued on the line, but Garza wasn't sure exactly what to make of it. He heard shouts, curses and questions for the most part, but they told him nothing. Even the most disciplined of soldiers sometimes panicked, and he couldn't call these men the best, by any means. Most of them wouldn't qualify as soldiers in the normal sense, but they were quick enough to shoot if they felt threatened—even if the threat was only in their minds.

Before he hit the panic button, Garza had to satisfy himself that it was warranted. He didn't want El Jefe thinking he was weak, a coward who grew faint and wet himself the first time trouble reared its head.

"Flavio!" he bawled. "Where are you, Flavio, goddammit?"

"Here, Enrique!" Coming up behind him in a rush, his second in command was winded, worried-looking.

Garza raised his voice to make it audible above the gunfire. "Who's responsible for this? What are they shooting at?"

Flavio shrugged expansively. "I don't—"

Whatever else he meant to say was smothered by the booming sound of an explosion. Garza spun in time to see a geyser shoot up from the farthest pit, where young men wearing shorts spent all day turning coca leaves to mulch. The blast sent half a dozen of them reeling, raining shredded leaves and muck upon them as they fell.

"That's a grenade!" Flavio said.

"Grenade? Our men don't have—"

The second blast erased all doubt. This one exploded in the middle of the camp, a puff of smoke and flame from nowhere. Garza ducked and heard the whine of shrapnel flying overhead.

He clutched the Armalite with white-knuckled, trembling hands, but he saw no targets, nothing but his own men scurrying around the compound, firing aimlessly into the trees that lay beyond. As Garza watched, one of the men jerked and fell, twitching, blood pulsing from a small wound in his chest.

It's time to panic now, he thought, and raced back toward his hut to use the radio.

KEELY ROSS PITCHED her second grenade—six left—and ducked back under cover as the camp's defenders sprayed the perimeter with automatic fire. Only the first of them had actually seen her, she believed, and he was dead now, but a stray round could prove every bit as lethal as a well-aimed shot.

The trick was making sure the other guys took all the

hits—and being careful not to kill the man they'd come to save, of course.

Thinking of Matt Cooper made her wonder if they'd come this far on a wild-goose chase. But they were in the middle of it now, and there was nothing to do but keep fighting as if her life depended on it. Because, in fact, it did.

Moving closer to the nearest buildings, Ross lined up a target in her rifle sights and hit him with a 3-round burst from forty feet. The 5.56 mm tumblers ripped through flesh and bone like churning blades and dropped him where he stood.

Another shooter came around the corner of the shed behind her target as the first man fell. He recoiled from the sight, but his reflexes weren't quick enough to save him. Ross squeezed off another burst and grimaced as the stranger's head exploded, the impact spinning him away and out of play.

Two weeks earlier, before she'd ever fired a shot in anger at another human being, this would have been inconceivable to Ross. This day, it almost seemed routine—and that troubled her.

She wasn't sure exactly what to look for. Any structure that could double as a cell and keep Cooper safe from prying eyes while his interrogators worked on him. It could be anything, a toolshed or a bunker. They'd have to take the place apart to satisfy themselves he wasn't here, and then—

A bullet whispered past her head, and Ross swung left to face the shooter, firing from the hip before she had her target clearly marked. The enemy recoiled, ducking for cover, but she caught him on the move and stitched him with a burst that opened him from hip to armpit, slamming him against the side wall of a hut that shuddered from the impact.

Check it out, she told herself, almost before another death had time to register. Ross charged on through the ferns and creepers, using the trees for cover from the others as she ran. Reaching the hut, she ducked behind it and worked her way around the north side of the eight-by-twelve structure. The hut had no windows, but if she could just reach the door—

Rounding the northeast corner, Ross discovered there was no fourth wall, no place for anyone to hide within the open shed. Equipment was stacked in there, some rakes and other gardening tools, gunnysacks labeled in Spanish that she couldn't read, a massive coil of nylon rope.

No prisoner. Another waste of time.

A spray of bullets raked the shed, punching through the corrugated metal walls and roof. Ross dodged and went to ground, hiding as best she could from the incoming fire. Tracking the source, she saw three shooters moving forward, fanning out to trap her and provide triangulated fire.

Or so they planned.

She spoiled it for them in a hurry, sighting on the foremost runner with her CAR-15 and dropping him midstride with a rising burst that left him dead before he hit the ground.

The other two sensed trouble, veering off in opposite directions, weapons blazing as they ran. It was a fair defense, but they were running for their lives with no time to stop and aim. As a result, they fired too high and wasted rounds that could have finished her.

Ross dropped the second runner with a spray of shots that cut his legs from under him. He fell across her line of fire, jerking and twisting as more bullets tore his flesh. She didn't overdo it, knowing he was finished or next to it as she swung away to track the third and last of her immediate opponents.

He was almost fast enough to nail her, but the instinct for survival worked against him. When he should have rushed her, firing for effect, the gunman turned away and tried to save himself with speed.

He showed her his back, and Ross took advantage of the lapse, lined up her shot and put him down.

Before the body finished twitching, she was on her feet and moving toward the next structure in camp. She had a job to do, had pledged to see it through, and fear of death was not enough to stop her.

Not this time, when she had come this far.

If Matt was here, she'd find him. If he wasn't—well, in that case, there'd be pure, unbridled hell to pay.

JACK GRIMALDI'S helicopter was a Bell LongRanger. It started life as a military aircraft, then went into retirement with a new paint job and registration numbers, stripped of the hardware it once carried under its nose.

Fortunately for Grimaldi, almost anything was available in Colombia for a price. Ten grand U.S. had reconnected the Bell's weapon system and mounted a .50-caliber gun beneath Grimaldi's feet, its adjustable fire selector set for a "slow" 1,000 rounds per minute to conserve ammunition.

With that monster, Grimaldi could have raked the drug compound himself—at least, until his ammo stash ran out— but there was no way he could check inside the different buildings from on high, no way to guarantee one of his bursts wouldn't gut Mack Bolan like a trophy deer.

So he'd made the delivery, two miles off target as agreed, and then retreated to his backup position, a preselected clearing on a mountaintop southeast of where Johnny and Ross would be making their first real contact with the local enemy. He didn't count the skirmish in Bello, outside Medellín, where they'd wasted two of Hector Santiago's men and taken a third one alive for interrogation. That was only a preliminary action, setting up the main event—or one of them, at least.

Whichever way it went, whether they found Bolan or not, Grimaldi knew there'd be more action in Colombia.

Unless they lost it all, right here and now.

Grimaldi didn't want to go there, so he concentrated on his instruments and on the chopper's two-way radio. His was tuned to a separate channel from the one Ross and Johnny used to communicate via their compact headsets. He didn't need the blow-by-blow from ground level to keep him on edge. It was enough that either one of them could reach him when they wanted to, when it was time for him to do his part.

As usual, extraction was the problem. They'd gone in with static lines, which reeled in automatically as Grimaldi was lifting up and out of the LZ, but pickups were a different story. For one thing, if they caught a break, there might be three to go, and the Bell's winch would only accommodate two at a time. That meant delays that could be fatal under fire, and there was only so much the Stony Man pilot could do to cover comrades on the ground while others were dangling like yo-yos from the chopper's belly.

If they scratched on finding Bolan, there could still be problems with the pickup. He was sitting on the only clear LZ for ten or fifteen miles around, and waiting for them there would only amplify the risks of a fighting withdrawal. They'd need pickup sooner, which meant skimming over the treetops and looking for daylight, someplace where Grimaldi could cast down his fishing lines and hope to snag a couple of live ones.

Using aerial photos, they'd selected two extraction sites. Grimaldi had coordinates for both locations memorized and plotted in his mental data bank. He needed only one short message from his comrades on the ground to make it work.

But if they couldn't send that message, they were well and truly screwed.

And if Grimaldi couldn't fix it, they'd agreed up front that he should burn the mother down.

Scorched earth, Johnny had told him, made him promise. *If it comes to that, scorched earth. I want your word.*

Grimaldi had agreed, reluctantly, though he had doubts concerning how much damage he could do with the .50-caliber Gatling gun and a 4,000-round ammunition reserve. Four minutes of sustained fire on target, all right, but there wasn't much he could do if his enemies scattered into the forest. The chopper couldn't hunt them there, and he couldn't really burn the mother down without explosives or incendiaries.

Still, something was better than nothing.

The Stony Man pilot would do what he could with the tools at hand—and maybe he'd come back for more when he'd had a chance to regroup.

For the moment, though, he was focused on winning, not losing. He wanted his friends out of there in one piece, with the precious cargo they'd come to retrieve.

All safe and sound, he thought, knowing the odds against it. But he beamed it to the universe regardless—*if there's anybody listening, please keep them safe and sound.*

GARZA WAS SO EXCITED that he nearly dropped the walkie-talkie on his first attempt, fumbling and catching it before it hit the floor. God help him if he broke it without sending for the reinforcements. Strangers wouldn't need to kill him, then. El Jefe would be pleased to do it for them, nice and slow, the kind of death that was protracted over days of agony.

He didn't break the walkie-talkie, though, and when he

barked out the call sign, the answer came back promptly. "Roger, Echo One. I read you, five-by-five."

Garza forgot the code and the procedure then. Fear and relief combined to start him babbling like a child with news to share. "It's happening!" he blurted out. "Guerrillas! They're attacking! Send the others now!"

He waited for a confirmation, then switched off the radio and left it on the folding table where he'd found it. There was no one else to call, no other help to summon. If the reinforcements came in time, he might survive.

Garza retrieved his Armalite and left the hut. Its thin walls offered nothing in the way of shelter from incoming rounds, and he could not return fire from an unseen enemy. Better to take his chances in the open, Garza thought—or else, to find a better hiding place.

New firing echoed from his left, and Garza dropped into a crouch, sweeping the compound with his rifle. No immediate targets presented themselves, unless he meant to fire on his own men, and they were close to that themselves, running every which way in a fury of pointless activity, firing at enemies who seemed to have no substance.

Garza edged his way around the hut that served as his quarters and command post while he was running the camp. He felt a need to get away, but when the reinforcements reached the compound, they'd be counting on him for direction. He could not desert them and his men, not if he wanted to survive El Jefe's wrath.

An inner voice commanded him to do something, assert himself somehow. But what could one man do amid the chaos that surrounded him? Without an enemy to fight, a target he could see and kill, what good was he to anyone?

A sound of helicopters roused him from his funk and

brought him to his feet. As he stared eastward, Garza saw the two aircraft, resembling flies at first, then growing larger by the moment as they homed in on the camp.

A few more minutes, Garza thought, and it would be all right.

The bullet struck him then, piercing his back below a shoulder blade and drilling through to exit from his chest. Falling, he didn't know it was a stray round that had entered through the north wall of his quarters and deflected just enough in passage through the empty rooms to find him quite by accident.

Fortunes of war.

Enrique Garza lay and listened to the helicopters coming closer, closer by the moment, fuming in the bitter irony that they would be too late to help him now. Whatever happened to the camp and his subordinates, he would never see it, never know. It might have made him laugh, if only he could breathe.

JOHNNY STEPPED OVER two fresh corpses, cleared the threshold of the structure they'd been guarding—and found nothing but a modest store of radio equipment, green and amber lights burning across the board.

Strike two.

"I've still got nothing," he informed the headset microphone. "One barracks left to check, and then—"

The sound of whirlybirds silenced him. One heartbeat, then another, and he knew it wasn't a mistake.

"Hear that?" he asked the microphone.

"Choppers," Ross answered him from somewhere on the far side of the camp.

"It isn't Jack," he said, confirming what they both knew.

"Backup." Her voice was grim. "How do we handle it?"

Plain logic told him there was only one recourse, no matter how it tortured him. "We're getting out," he told her. "Do it now. I'll tell Jack that it's LZ-1."

"Roger. I'm on my way."

A burst of automatic fire from her approximate position told him Ross had dealt with some obstruction to her flight. He was busy changing frequencies, already moving toward the tree line as he spoke into the air once more.

"Ground Hog to Flyboy. Do you read me?"

"Five by five," Grimaldi answered, no lag time to speak of.

"We've got party crashers coming in," he said. "Airborne. We're bailing out for LZ-1 right now."

"No package?" He could hear the tension in Grimaldi's voice.

"Nothing," Johnny replied. "It's got a setup smell."

"Damn it! All right, I'm on my way to LZ-1. Be there ahead of you, with any luck."

"Out."

Johnny was about to switch the frequency again, to stay in touch with Ross, when two armed sentries blocked his path. For all their paramilitary bearing, they were visibly surprised to meet him, both of them recoiling, leveling their weapons for a point-blank spray.

He didn't give them time. Rushing the pair of them, Johnny lashed out with the butt of his rifle, clubbing the one on his left in the face. The blow staggered his opponent and made him gasp aloud in pain. Johnny followed through the move, a sweep that put the carbine's muzzle inches from the second shooter's head as Johnny squeezed the trigger and unleashed a 4-round burst.

The gunner's face disintegrated, crimson mist replacing startled features as he toppled backward in a boneless sprawl. Johnny kept charging, whipping the carbine back around and slamming its butt into the other lookout's teeth. The guard squeezed off a shot as he was falling, but it gouged a divot from the earth at Johnny's feet. When Johnny answered with a double-tap at point-blank range, his muzzle-flash left scorch marks on the target's khaki shirt.

He ran before anyone else could home in on the sounds of battle and come looking for a piece of the action. Behind him, the sound of the choppers was closer, bearing down on him at something like a hundred miles per hour. Johnny didn't know if they would touch down in the camp or try to hunt him from the air, but either way he knew the fight had just begun.

It was a setup all along, he thought, and wondered how the man in charge had pulled it off. Of course, he would've known that someone would come looking for his captive and he had to have made allowances. Feeding disinformation to his own troops, maybe, so that any one of them who let it slip would tell the enemy precisely what El Jefe wanted them to hear.

It isn't over yet, Johnny thought, as he hammered through the forest in a sprint.

Their adversary hadn't reckoned on one seasoned jungle fighter and a damned fast learner with survival skills second to none. He hadn't reckoned on Grimaldi, either, winging in to fetch them in a chopper of his own, with a surprise in store for anyone who tried to head him off.

Running, the burn already penetrating his lungs and muscles, Johnny wondered whether it would be enough to see them through alive.

Charging downhill, he saw the twisted root a split second before it snagged his foot and sent him tumbling through an awkward somersault, clutching the rifle to his chest and giving in to gravity as it drew him bouncing down the mountainside.

2

Grimaldi had the Bell LongRanger airborne seconds after he finished talking to Johnny. He hadn't revved up the whirly-bird during their brief conversation, because he feared missing whatever the kid had to say. When the numbers were tight and lives were riding on the line, there was no such thing as a minor mistake.

Grimaldi's clearing was four miles from the camp and three miles from the point they had designated LZ-1. The second pickup point was a full mile south of LZ-1, and while the distance didn't sound like much in idle conversation, it seemed to stretch forever when you were down in the midst of it, running for your life over hostile, unfamiliar terrain.

So he would be there, waiting for them when they reached the clearing. He wouldn't leave them hanging, wondering if something had gone wrong.

Unless, of course, something did.

The chopper was in good form, lifting smoothly, hovering as ordered, then banking away toward the point his friends were making for, giving it everything they had. Grimaldi hoped the hunters weren't too close behind them, weren't too good at what they were supposed to do.

The set had been a trap. He saw that now, and it had worried him when they were planning the incursion. He had mentioned it, in fact, but they had all agreed—himself included—that it was worth the risk to rescue Bolan.

If they found him, it was worth the risk. In this case, though, it seemed they had been hooked and reeled in by a fisherman who knew his game.

Grimaldi didn't stop to think about the kind of man and mind required to play that way. To plant false information with his men and hope that one of them was captured, tortured, forced to spill his guts before he died.

It took a hard man, and then some, to sacrifice his own players like that. Ruthless. Determined. As cold as ice.

Your average drug lord, sure.

Today we turn the trap around, Grimaldi thought, and instantly wished there was something made of wood inside the chopper's cockpit, something he could knock on for good luck. He harbored no more superstition than the average combat pilot, but he knew it couldn't hurt to hedge his bets, either.

There was a chance the trap might be too good, too tight. They might not make it out, in which case—what?

Grimaldi hadn't thought that far ahead. It went against his grain, smacking of defeatism, but he thought about it now, winging over the treetops at maximum speed.

What happened if they all went down in flames this afternoon?

The silence would tip Hal Brognola at Justice, but not for a while. Several hours, at least, would elapse before Hal started putting two and two together. And from there? A hand off to some other team, presumably—maybe guys Grimaldi knew. They'd have to start from scratch, or pretty close, but they would do the job eventually.

Let's get it right the first time, he thought.

He was almost there, a few miles was not much at all when he was airborne and traveling 130 miles per hour. The blink of an eye, really, and then he was circling the clearing below, knowing he was too damned early for the runners to be waiting. Knowing, too, that if he stayed on post above the pickup point, he risked drawing heat to his friends as surely as if they had homing devices clipped to their cammo fatigues.

He took the Bell LongRanger up and out of there, breaking precious visual contact, trusting his radio to tell him when Johnny and Ross reached the clearing and needed his help. He was sweating it out now, but that was the price of a seat at the table. You paid for the privilege of playing in blood, sweat and tears.

Just make it someone else's blood today, he thought, circling. Waiting. The whisper-hiss of silence in his ears was maddening.

"Come on," he urged his unseen comrades, somewhere in the woods below. "Come on! Don't leave me hanging here."

But there was no reply.

ROSS DIDN'T KNOW if Johnny was in front of her, or still somewhere behind. They hadn't planned a rendezvous when they were bailing out, because it would have cost them precious time and left them vulnerable to the shooters who were hunting them.

And they were there. She had no doubt of it.

Ross couldn't hear them yet, but that meant nothing. She was making so much noise herself, a troupe of monkeys could have been pursuing her and she wouldn't have known until she was overtaken. Forget that stuff about a soldier's silent progress through the forest. Silence and speed were two sides of a coin for Ross. She couldn't have them both faceup at once.

Halfway to LZ-1, the doubts began to nag at her. If Johnny was behind her, should she stop and wait for him? What if he'd been cut off, or ambushed?

No, she told herself. No shooting back there, yet. I would've heard gunfire at least.

But what if he was hurt or cut off by the enemy? Maybe the hunters didn't know it yet, but they had leapfrogged Johnny somehow and were blocking his approach to LZ-1. What then?

Nothing, Ross thought. She'd done all right the last two weeks, with fighting for her life on various examples of terrain, but she wasn't a tracker or trailblazer. She'd never find Johnny, at least not in time. And while she was messing around in the woods, she would be hanging Jack Grimaldi out to dry.

And what if Johnny got out first, if he was somewhere ahead of her in the forest and making less noise in his flight? In that case, any doubling back would work against them both, jeopardizing Ross's life for nothing, while Johnny stalled at the pickup point, waiting for her to arrive.

He wasn't supposed to do that, in theory, but she knew the way his mind worked. Leaving her behind, on top of failing to retrieve Cooper, would be more than he could stand. Not only because they'd forged an intimate connection in the past few days, but because they were on the same side.

It damn near killed Johnny to leave a comrade behind in the heat of battle. She and Grimaldi had been forced to drag him away from the Nassau hotel where Cooper was captured. They were compelled to stop him by force from throwing his life out the window on a dead-end rescue mission. Now, with

Grimaldi in the air and far out of reach, there'd be no one to stop Johnny from lingering if she was late at LZ-1.

No one to save him from himself.

Ross paused, just long enough to strain her ears for any sound of movement in the woods behind her. Somewhere overhead, she heard a helicopter slapping at the air—or was it more than one? Were the hunters hopscotching around them to cut off retreat?

What would Grimaldi do if he met them in the air?

While she was standing there, the sharp sound of a raised voice reached her ears. It didn't last, cut off almost before it sounded, but there was no mistaking it. Ross didn't think it had been Johnny's voice, but if she'd had to bet a life on it she wouldn't have been sure.

Most likely it was one of her pursuers from the compound. Something had surprised him, maybe fatally, she thought. The noise was not repeated, and she still heard no gunfire.

She ran, feeling the urge to sob with every jolting step she took. Fighting was one thing, even face-to-face. But running was different, especially when she didn't know if any of her friends were still alive.

How far to LZ-1?

Maybe another quarter of a mile.

Ross focused on her goal and tried hard not to think about the hunters coming up behind her, thirsty for her blood.

TOMAS AGUIRRE WIPED the long blade of his knife on the leg of his cammo fatigue pants, then sheathed it. At his feet, the body of Sancho Jimenez still quivered, blood pulsing darkly from the open chasm of his throat.

"I said no noise," he told the others, speaking in a whisper that was barely audible at fifteen feet. "I meant no noise!"

The others nodded, eyes wide, their weapons clutched in nervous hands. Beside Jimenez lay the thrashing, severed body of the viper that had startled him and wrenched a cry of warning from his lips.

It was the last sound he would ever make.

"All right, then," Aguirre said. "If we understand one another now, move out!" That whisper, as cold as death and twice as frightening.

Tomas Aguirre placed no faith in loyalty. He knew that killers served a chosen master out of greed or fear. Combining those two elements strengthened the master's hold, but fear should always have the stronger grip, in Aguirre's opinion. He had lost a man, but the remaining seven on his team would keep their damned mouths shut no matter what befell them, whether they stepped into a nest of stinging scorpions or someone set their pants on fire.

Silence was truly golden in a hunt like this, and if he couldn't make their footsteps silent in the clutching forest undergrowth, Aguirre could at least make sure they didn't chatter like a band of children skipping through a picnic ground on holiday.

They were a good deal closer to the enemy. He knew that much, at least, if not the names and number of his targets. There were signs available, for those with eyes to read them, and Aguirre had a tracker's skill. At least two runners were in front of him, and while he had expected more, Aguirre would be satisfied with two scalps on his belt, if there were no more to be had.

His orders had been simple: stop the raiders if and when they showed themselves. Take one alive, if possible, but make sure none escaped at any cost. Bring back the hands and any personal effects.

Simple.

It fell to his discretion whether those he sought would live or die. That's how Aguirre liked it. He would make an effort to keep one alive, but how much effort was another question. Anything could happen once the battle had been joined. Who knew what might become of those who challenged him?

The guards posted around the camp were useless, peasants who'd been handed weapons and some minimal authority, so full of themselves that they felt invincible—until the bullets started flying. That was when they fell apart, and men like Aguirre had to clean up their mess.

Aguirre hesitated, checking the forest signs in front of him. One of the men he sought had fallen here, it seemed, rolling downhill for some considerable distance. Aguirre wished him pain and injury. It would make the hunt that much simpler, the kill that much quicker. Or perhaps, if this one was hurt badly enough, they could drag him along as a prisoner of war.

Aguirre slowed his pace, tracking the signs, watching to see when and where his clumsy quarry had broken the fall. He hoped the stupid bastard hadn't rolled all the way down the side of the mountain and into the valley below. That would mean—

A sudden blaze of gunfire sent Tomas Aguirre diving headlong to the forest floor. He rolled behind the nearest tree while bullets fanned the air above him, striking bark and human flesh. One of his men cried out in pain—too late to slice the bastard now—and went down in a thrashing heap.

Aguirre clutched his weapon, thinking fast, while gunfire echoed back and forth among the trees. He didn't know how many of the enemy he faced, or where they were. The only thing Aguirre could be sure of was that sitting still meant death.

And so, he broke his own first rule.

"Kill them!" he called out sharply, to those of his men who were still on their feet. "Kill them all!"

JOHNNY HAD MISSED the point man, but he didn't let it rattle him. He needed to stop all of them, and if his first rounds took out the second or third man in line, that was simply the luck of the draw. Seven remained, by his hasty head count, and he still had some wet work to do.

The fall had shaken him, left Johnny cut and bruised all over, but he hadn't broken anything and all his limbs were functional. The loss of time hurt worse than any dings and scrapes he'd suffered, rolling down the mountainside, and there'd been only one way he could think to make it up.

Ambush.

If he'd kept running, tried to make up time, there was a chance they'd have missed him, but he didn't like the odds. More to the point, he didn't relish dying here and leaving Keely Ross to Santiago's men, knowing she'd wait for him at LZ-1 instead of lifting off with Jack and leaving him behind.

A bullet struck the tree beside his face, spraying his cheek with ragged shards of bark. Wincing, he found the shooter with his gunsights, tracked him on the run and hit him with a short burst that drilled home beneath an upraised arm to puncture lungs, heart, liver and the rest of it.

Two down, the survivors—all firing at him now, or most of them, as Johnny ducked and dodged. He palmed a frag grenade and yanked the pin. He pitched the bomb upslope against the pull of gravity, giving it force enough to get there without falling back into his lap.

One of the shooters saw it coming, called a warning to his pals and broke from cover when it would have served him better to stay put. Three seconds later, the explosion hurled the soldier face first, with crushing impact, into a tree trunk, while the shrapnel peppered him and pinned him there.

The others seemed to roll with it, but they were moving, cautiously advancing, trying hard to circle Johnny and cut him off. He tracked the nearest of them, ready with his shot until the target ducked behind a tree and left him staring at thin air.

Just then, one of the shooters on his right cut loose and raked the trunk that sheltered Johnny. Dropping to his knees, Johnny decided it was time to take a chance. Retreating several yards, he kept the tree between himself and immediate danger, but he left himself exposed to flankers. There was logic to it, but unless it worked, no one would ever know.

When he had eased back far enough in a straight line, Johnny rolled out to his right, the CAR-15 ready and braced against his shoulder. Sighting took a fraction of a second, and the shooter never saw it coming as Johnny hit him with a rising burst of 5.56 mm man-stoppers.

The remaining gunners startled him by rushing all at once, as if someone had given them a signal, but he could've sworn there'd been no spoken word. Hand signals, maybe, or some prearranged decision, but there wasn't any time to think about it as the skirmish line advanced, the hardforce firing at once.

Instinct made him lob another frag grenade toward the center of their line, where two of the shooters were closest together. Before it exploded, Johnny had lined up the guy on his left and punched four rounds through his scrawny chest, dropping the shooter in his tracks. A heartbeat later, the grenade went off and all he heard was screaming filtered through the echo of its blast.

Johnny was moving, even as the shock wave rippled through the trees and shrapnel sang around him. He knew the last man had been far enough away to miss the blast entirely, or to ride it out with only minor injury. Smart money said he would keep coming, and if that was wrong—well, there was still no harm in being careful, was there?

Johnny hunkered down within the lightning-scarred trunk of a huge, ancient tree, hoping no deadly snake had shared the same idea. He waited, skin crawling, until he heard footsteps approaching, crunching over leaves. One man by the sound of it, taking his time.

But not enough to save himself.

A moment later, the man stood in front of Johnny, scanning the downslope, wrinkling his forehead in perplexity. "Where are you, gringo?" he whispered to himself.

Right here, Johnny thought—and shot him in the back.

Rising, Johnny checked the battlefield and found no enemies still standing. There was time to reach the LZ if he was quick about it, but—

The helicopter sounded closer than it should have, and he knew instinctively it wasn't Grimaldi. Still hunting me, he thought. They're not done yet.

And with that thought in mind, he sprinted downhill, toward LZ-1.

HOW DID THEY GET in front of me? Ross asked herself.

She knew the answer even as the thought took shape. One of the choppers had to have flown ahead and dropped an interception team, as she had feared. They couldn't know where she was going, but it didn't take a military genius to leapfrog a runner and put soldiers in her path.

Ross would have done the same herself if the positions were reversed—and if she'd had any soldiers to spare. As it was, she was fresh out of allies, at least any ones she could see. Her two-way radio still worked, as far as she could tell, but what was the point in broadcasting her dilemma? She'd heard the gunfire behind her and reckoned Johnny had to be up to his ass in alligators, fighting for his life.

Unless he's dead, she thought, then squelched that one before it could take hold.

Ross knew what she had to do.

She checked the magazine on her assault rifle, found it nearly empty and replaced it with a fresh one. She didn't bother fiddling with the pistol. She knew it was cocked and locked, ready to go. She still had five grenades left and her combat knife. The bastards wouldn't take her easily.

They wouldn't take her alive.

Ross heard the hostiles moving closer, but she didn't plan to wait for them. There was nothing special about her present location, in terms of defensive advantages. She might as well keep moving, cautiously, and make some progress toward the pickup point. She had to at least try.

She took her time walking downhill, not rushing into it. If the hunters had already heard her, they gave no sign of it. Their discipline was shoddy. She heard them talking back and forth in Spanish as they swept the mountainside. Ross didn't know if it was a calculated tactic, designed to spook their quarry, or if they were simply lousy at their job.

In either case, she didn't plan to let them get away with it.

After another ten or fifteen yards, she found her spot. It was a freak of nature. One tree had long ago fallen against another, which had then absorbed the weight of the first tree and grown around it somehow, to create a piece of living statuary in the forest, both enchanting and grotesque.

More to the point, it granted decent cover.

Ross wormed underneath it, smelling mud and rotted leaves. The forests here were all deciduous, no evergreens, no fresh smell in the air. She always had the sense that death was close at hand—and now it truly was.

Her adversaries came on through the trees, still talking when they felt like it, but less than earlier. Perhaps they had a sense of foreboding, but it hadn't reached them soon enough. They were already visible to Ross from where she lay concealed, watching them over her rifle sights.

She had them now.

"All right," she whispered, scarcely breathing, as her index finger tightened on the rifle's trigger. "Come and get it."

THE HELICOPTERS ALMOST took Grimaldi by surprise. He'd guessed they had to be flying in reinforcements, or else the backup wouldn't have surprised Johnny and Ross. Still, he was thinking that they'd drop their soldiers at the compound, then pull back and wait it out as he had, since the forest down below gave them no opportunity for proper air support.

But he'd been wrong.

They obviously weren't content to send ground pounders after his companions, when they had a chance to hunt them from the air. It was a dicey proposition, even if they had some kind of heat seekers on board, but they couldn't have known how risky the job was about to become.

Grimaldi couldn't tell from a distance if the other two choppers were armed, and he didn't give a damn. They stood between him and the pickup he'd promised to make, and that was enough.

They had to go.

The LongRanger's weapon system was already armed and ready to rock. Grimaldi chose the closer of the helicopters as his first target, noting on the approach that it was an Aérospatiale 322 Super Puma, built to carry as many as twenty-one passengers. He hoped the pilot hadn't dropped that many shooters in the woods below—much less double the number—but there was no one to ask, no way to find out.

Just do what you can, said the voice in his head.

Take 'em out.

The Super Puma's pilot didn't see him coming. Grimaldi supposed he was watching the treetops, maybe talking to his ground force on the two-way radio, but he should have spared a moment to examine his immediate surroundings. If he had, the first blast from Grimaldi's GAU/19A Gatling gun might not have done the damage that it did.

He tried to keep it short and sweet, not wasting ammunition when the piece devoured rounds at a rate of seventeen per second. Just a featherlight touch on the trigger, holding steady in the Bell, and he watched bullets slash through the target's tail section, damn near sawing it off in midair.

The other pilot didn't know what hit him, and he had no chance to recover. A heartbeat after Grimaldi fired, the big chopper started to spin, its nearly severed tail section wobbling crazily, no help at all with propulsion or steering. Grimaldi could have finished it with a another burst to the cockpit, but he didn't bother. The ship was going down, and the Stony Man pilot couldn't have cared less whether the pilot lived or not. Anyone aboard the crippled whirlybird was in for the ride of his life, with a probable fiery death waiting below.

Grimaldi focused his full attention on the second chopper now. Its pilot had observed his comrade's fate, or maybe heard the loser squealing on his radio, but either way Grimaldi knew the second chopper wouldn't be an easy kill. Whether the pilot would run or stand his ground and fight was an open question, though.

Grimaldi skimmed across the treetops, racing toward his

target, noting that the second airship made no effort to avoid him. This one was a Hughes 500, smaller than the Super Puma, with maximum seating for six. That part encouraged Grimaldi, but he also knew the smaller, lighter whirlybird might out-maneuver his own if it had a savvy pilot in the cockpit.

"Okay, then," he muttered. "Let's see what you've got."

It turned out to be a rifleman in the copilot's seat. Not much, as airborne defenses went, but it was very nearly good enough to take out Grimaldi. He was racing headlong toward the target when the little chopper swung around broadside, and he saw the shooter sighting on him through the open doorway. Grimaldi was nearly too late as he hauled back on the joystick to gain altitude, hearing bullets crack against the Plexiglas in front of him and hammer at the fuselage below.

The turkey shoot had turned into a dogfight, and it took Grimaldi the better part of five long minutes to trick his op-ponent, letting the enemy pilot and shooter believe he'd been shaken or wounded, letting the smaller ship come up behind him for the killing shot.

Only then, when it was lined up and ready to strike, did Grimaldi spring his do-or-die trap, cutting back his speed until the Bell LongRanger nearly stalled and started dropping like a stone. The pilot dogging him was unprepared and swept past him in an instant, roaring overhead. That was when he gunned it, climbing swiftly, hoping he could find his mark be-fore the smaller, faster bird turned.

One instant he was falling toward the treetops, and the next he was soaring. Feeling the roller-coaster rush that had made him start flying in the first place, Grimaldi locked his sights onto the startled enemy's aircraft. This time, he didn't play games with the trigger, hosing his mark for a good fif-teen seconds before he let go.

Sixty yards in front of him, the little Hughes seemed to disintegrate, shattered and shredded by fifteen hundred armor-piercing .50-caliber rounds traveling at 2,900 feet per second. Grimaldi was banking away by the time it exploded, raining fire and shattered wreckage on the forest below.

He was late for the pickup. He wondered if there'd be anybody there when he arrived.

"YOU MADE IT," Ross said as he came through the trees, approaching LZ-1. Johnny noted surprise in her voice.

"You, too."

"Touch and go," she told him. "Any tails left?"

Johnny shook his head. "I saw the ones they dropped ahead of us."

"They weren't so tough."

"You're bleeding."

Ross plucked at the torn left sleeve of her fatigue blouse. "It's nothing. Just a graze."

"We'll take care of it anyway."

"If Jack shows up, you mean."

Johnny had heard the firing and explosions that signaled an aerial dogfight. He didn't want to think about Grimaldi smoldering in twisted wreckage on the forest floor, but it was possible. They'd have to wait and see.

"He's late," Ross noted, glancing at the sky revealed above the clearing they had designated LZ-1.

"We've still got time."

"How much?"

He couldn't answer that one honestly. Survivors at the compound might send out another scouting party if the hunters didn't check in via radio—or maybe they'd already gotten signals telling them the play had gone to hell. How long before they hit the trail and covered the few miles to LZ-1?

"He'll be here," Johnny said, hoping Grimaldi didn't make him out a liar in the end.

"Somebody's coming, anyway," Ross said. She raised her weapon, muzzle angled toward the blue sky.

He heard the chopper now, approaching, and he had to wonder whether it was Jack or yet another load of hunters coming to finish what the others had started. If they came down on static lines, Johnny guessed he and Ross could teach them a lesson in applied gravity. But if the chopper was a gunship...

He recognized the Bell LongRanger, even from below. Grimaldi's voice was frosting on the cake. "Somebody call a cab?" he asked.

"We're ready any time you are," Johnny replied.

"Okay, then. Let's go fishing."

The static lines began their long, jerky descent, fast-release harnesses dangling from the end of each. It took only a minute for the lines to reach their full extension, but it seemed ten times that long in Johnny's mind. He stood watch with his CAR-15 while Ross hooked up her rigging, then got buckled in himself while she covered the tree line.

"Ready," he announced, and in another second they were airborne, Grimaldi rising at the same time he reeled in the lines. It was a dizzying ascent, quite different from the drop, and Johnny felt as if he'd left a portion of himself behind.

His brother, that would be.

"Hold on," he told the treetops, as they fell away beneath his boots. And once again. "Hold on, damn it. We haven't given up."

3

Medellín, Colombia

"It seems your plan was not successful, Hector." Semyon Borodin smiled as he spoke, clearly taking pleasure from his host's discomfort.

"It was sound in theory," Santiago replied. He was determined not to let the Russian anger him—at least until the time was right. "We had logistics problems, though."

"That's when your men get killed and all your helicopters get shot down, I take it." The Russian smirked. "Everywhere I go, these days, it seems my friends have these *logistics problems.*"

"You should be more careful, in that case," Santiago suggested. "A superstitious man might think you brought the bad luck with you. He might hold the harbinger responsible."

Borodin's smile quickly faded. "I am grateful in that case," he said, "that you are not a superstitious man, Hector."

"Don't be so sure. I come from peasant stock, the same as you. Fine houses, cars and clothing may define a man, but they don't change the way he thinks, the way he feels inside."

The Russian's face had colored slightly at the mention of his peasant roots, but he took it in stride. "With all respect, my friend, I think you're wrong. I know that I, for one, have greatly changed since the days when I picked pockets and rolled filthy drunks for spare change. I've come up in the world. Haven't you?"

It was a challenge. Santiago saw that, but he would only rise so far toward the bait. "Indeed," he said, "but it's the same world I was born in, run by the same corrupt people."

Borodin smiled again. "Ah, perhaps. But now you corrupt them, instead of playing errand boy."

"It cuts both ways. I'm sure you know that, Semyon. Only if our plan succeeds in full will we be truly free. And at the moment, frankly, I have doubts."

"It's only natural," the Russian said. "If you want to pull out—"

And leave another share for you, Santiago thought, even as he interrupted. "No, I didn't say that. I'm concerned, however, that we're taking many losses without gaining anything. Already, the Americans are out."

"They'll come back with their hands out soon enough," Borodin said. "They need our product more than we need their distributors. Just give them time to pick another goombah, and you'll hear them knocking at the door with hat in hand."

"You're very smug."

"It's called self-confidence, Hector."

"Too much of that can be a fatal flaw."

"I know the difference, believe me. Are the others coming soon?" the Russian asked.

"They should be here within the next half hour or so."

Santiago had scheduled a meeting of all concerned partners to discuss the latest outbreak of violence. He expected to take heat for it, the "good" news being that only his personal soldiers were dead. As for the rest—

"They'll want to hear about the prisoner," Borodin said, reading his mind.

"And you will tell them…what, Semyon?"

"That he's been stubborn, but I'm working on it."

"Ah. Logistical problems?"

The Russian's smile was icy. "I still have a few tricks up my sleeve."

"Of course. But if you need help, Semyon, by all means feel free to borrow Eduardo. He works wonders on stubborn tongues."

"Maybe later. Has there been any sign of Tripp?" Borodin asked, changing the subject.

Garrett Tripp, their mercenary security chief and acting officer in charge of the cartel's private army, had vanished after his latest defeat at the hands of unknown opponents. Santiago didn't know if Tripp was dead, or if he'd grasped the price of failure and fled for his life.

"Not yet," the Colombian answered simply. "I'm pursuing inquiries."

"Of course. In his absence, I think there's a void to be filled."

Santiago sipped his wine, frowning. Borodin had been angling for a bigger piece of the action almost from day one, backbiting and undercutting Tripp's authority at every given opportunity. Santiago would not have been surprised to learn that the Russian was responsible for some of their recent problems—except that he had also been a target, nearly killed himself, in Nassau.

"We can discuss such matters when we're all assembled, yes? It's the way things are done in civilized society."

"Since when has our society been civilized?" Borodin asked, mocking him.

The Russian's smile was fierce, almost gleeful. For the first time during their association, Santiago wondered whether Borodin was clinically insane.

MACK BOLAN WASN'T sleeping, but a casual observer might have thought he was. In fact, he'd reached a mental state just short of sleep, his body relaxed to the extent pain would allow it, a portion of his groggy mind at rest while the remainder grappled with insistent questions still unanswered.

How much longer could he last?

Was there a chance to get away?

Perhaps to die?

The last two questions now had answers, anyway. He wasn't going anywhere unless his captors moved him, and he was surviving at their sufferance, until they finished with him and grew tired of playing cat-and-mouse. So far, for all their sadistic ingenuity, they hadn't inflicted any crippling or life-threatening injuries. And they had told him, early on in the interrogation, that there was a doctor standing by to make sure Bolan didn't cheat them by dying ahead of their schedule.

They didn't know his name, of course. He'd given them the Matt Cooper cover story after several hours of encouragement, and while he didn't think the men in charge believed it for a second, they had moved on to the nature of his mission, who employed him, what they wanted—all the questions he could not afford to answer.

In the end, he knew, there'd be no stopping them from breaching his defenses, dragging everything he knew or could imagine from his mind in one long scream. Bolan possessed a high pain threshold, but it wasn't infinite. No one was. He knew the break was coming, just as surely as he drew one breath after another.

He hadn't tried to piss them off yet, goading them toward lethal loss of self-control, but maybe it was time to start. He guessed that if there'd been help coming, it should have arrived by now. Johnny had no ready way to find him. Hell, for all Bolan knew, his brother might be dead by now. And if that was the case—

He would see how it went in the next inevitable round of interrogation. A man couldn't suffocate by simply holding his breath—Mother Nature didn't allow it—but there might be a way to push his inquisitors over the edge, make them angry enough that they would—

Footsteps.

Bolan kept his eyes closed, savoring the last few seconds of tranquility before they went to work on him again. What would it be this time? Electric shock or open flame? Blunt force or pointed instruments? Dry ice or scalding liquid?

Pain was all the same, he had decided. Whether dull or sharp, acute or chronic, it was all part of the same debilitating fabric that surrounded him and promised ultimately to destroy him.

The door opened behind him, a trick to keep him guessing about who had entered, where the next blow was coming from. It would have been more effective, though, if his visitor had laid off the trademark sickly sweet cologne.

"You've suffered much," said the Colombian who called himself simply Eduardo. He hadn't laid a hand on Bolan yet, but he was always there for the interrogation sessions, watching and waiting. "You've been lucky so far."

"All a matter of perspective," Bolan answered.

"Perhaps. But your luck won't last much longer."

Bolan didn't answer. There seemed to be no point.

Frowning, Eduardo prodded him. "Do you know why?"

The shrug was painful, but Bolan managed. "I suppose you're here to tell me."

"*Sí.* That's right. Your luck will run out soon because they're giving you to me."

"An early Christmas present?"

"Joke while you're still able, gringo." Eduardo's smile was feral, his foul breath stronger than the sweet cologne. "So far, you've been handled by clumsy amateurs. You won't last an hour with me."

"I'm surprised," Bolan told him.

Eduardo cocked an eyebrow. "So? You doubt me?"

Another painful shrug. "I'm just surprised you'd want to rush it. That can't be much fun for a sick, twisted bastard like you."

Eduardo stiffened, the color draining from his narrow face before it came back in a crimson wave. Instead of striking Bolan, he took a moment, searching for his self-control and finding it. Bolan watched him relax, the grim smile coming back.

"You're clever, for a stinking gringo, but you won't get off so easily. Before I'm done, you'll beg for death. You'll give me everything I want, and more."

THE CONFERENCE ROOM was thirty feet by twelve, a long rectangle with a highly polished table in the middle of it, ringed by high-backed swivel chairs. Because two members of the cartel were not present in the flesh, a pair of thirty-six-inch televisions had been set up at their places, tuned to satellite transmissions from abroad. Dante Ambrosio was still in Sicily, and Sun Zu-wang had not left Nassau when the final round of shooting started. They joined the others by benefit of high technology.

The rest of those assembled were familiar faces. Hector Santiago sat at the head of the table, fulfilling his role as the host. The seat immediately to his right was empty, since his number two had died in Nassau hours earlier. To his left sat the Yakuza delegation, Kenji Tanaka and Tomichi Kano. Across the table from the Japanese sat Borodin and his second in command, Nicolai Yurochka. Beyond them, more empty seats marked the places where the American crime lords would sit, if they were still alive. Maxwell Reed seemed out of place and lonely at the far end of the table, but his military bearing kept him ramrod straight, hands folded on the table before him.

"Welcome, all of you," Santiago began. "We've lost many in the past two weeks. From America, Vincent Ruggero and Joseph DeMitri, with many of their soldiers. In Panama, the brave associates of Mr. Sun, who joins us now by satellite. And finally, in Nassau, my friend Pablo Aznar."

"And more today," Borodin interrupted him. "Don't forget that."

"I've forgotten nothing," Santiago replied stiffly. "Every death reminds me of how far we've come—and how far we still have to go."

"If I may say," Reed piped up from the far end of the table, "it begins to feel as if we're running out of time."

"Not yet, I trust," Santiago replied. "Our troops are still making progress on Isla de Victoria, are they not?"

"Slow advances at best," Reed answered. "I had hoped to be within reach of the capital by now."

"Plans change," Santiago suggested.

"And always for the worse, it seems," Borodin chimed in, flashing his vulpine smile. The crazy smile. "We've had nothing but setbacks the past two weeks. I daresay Mr. Reed—I mean, Mr. President—has suffered fewer losses on the battlefield than we have in our own backyards."

"Not your backyard," Sun reminded Borodin. His lips were slightly out of synch with his voice, thanks to some quirk of the satellite's transmission. It made him resemble a character in a poorly dubbed kung-fu movie.

"You think I've had no losses just because these bastards aren't hunting in Moscow? The night before last I was nearly killed in my own hotel room, where I was assured I'd be safe. I have men dead in Nassau whose bodies I don't dare to claim."

"We've all suffered loss," Santiago interjected. As he spoke, his eyes flicked toward the second television screen, filled with Don Ambrosio's face, and he thought, *most of us, at least.* "We need to place the blame where it belongs, on the heads of our enemies."

"Who," Tanaka said, "I understand you still have not identified."

"We have a prisoner," Santiago explained, trusting that all of them had heard the news by now. "Unfortunately, he has so far managed to resist interrogation."

"What? How is that possible?" Don Ambrosio demanded. "You must be coddling him!"

"In fact, I've left the questioning to our Russian friends... so far."

Borodin squirmed in the spotlight. "It's true he's been a tough nut to crack," the Russian admitted, "but I'll break him today."

"And if you don't, what then?" Sun asked.

"I have a specialist on staff," Santiago told them. "He's on standby, ready to step in at any time."

"Why wait?" Tanaka asked. "If nothing else has worked so far?"

"I captured him," Borodin said, puffing out his chest. "It should be me who questions him."

"We are supposed to be collaborating, not competing," Sun reminded him.

The Russian scowled. "Of course, if everyone insists, I won't object."

"A wise decision, beneficial to us all," Santiago said.

Maxwell Reed cleared his throat. "If I may interrupt again, with one more question?"

"Of course, Mr. President. By all means, what is it?"

"I see that Mr. Tripp is not among us. Can you tell us where he is?"

The door opened so quietly that Santiago didn't hear it, but he couldn't miss the voice that answered in his place.

"I'm here," Garrett Tripp said. "Right here."

COMING IN WAS the King Kong risk of all time, but Garrett Tripp had calculated that it was also the best way to keep himself alive. Just getting past the drug lord's guards had been a gamble, but he'd bet against himself that Santiago wouldn't waste time briefing all his local shooters to be wary of a man they'd seen a hundred times before, when Santiago himself never thought Tripp would drop by for coffee.

And he had been right.

So far, so good.

Now, as he traveled the length of the conference room with every eye boring into him and the two remote viewers asking questions from their TV monitors, Tripp knew the hard part of the game still lay in front of him. Getting past the sentries had been child's play. A word from Santiago now, and the shooters would swarm like hornets, maybe drag him off to one of Eduardo's operating rooms.

"Sorry I'm late," he told the room. "I nearly got my ass shot off in Nassau, and by the time the smoke cleared, everyone else had bailed out. I had to pull some strings to find out where you'd gone."

"And here you are," Borodin said, sneering. "Alive and well."

"It was touch-and-go for a while," Tripp replied.

"But you survived," Santiago said. "Unlike my *segundo* and so many of my men. Nearly two days without a word."

Here was the part where Tripp knew he was really tempting fate. "I couldn't call," he said, "until I found out whether any of you thought I had a hand in what went down."

Borodin blinked once in surprise. "You have good instincts, Mr. Tripp," he admitted. "I, for one, have asked that question and received no satisfactory reply."

"Exactly," Tripp replied, watching his masters stiffen all around the table. "And I couldn't answer you until I found out who's been ragging on us for the past two weeks."

"And now you know?" The tone of Santiago's voice was frankly skeptical.

"Not all of it, but maybe just enough to get them off our backs."

While they were staring at him, Tripp pulled out the chair reserved for him and sat in it. To his left, the muttering from the TVs had stopped.

"We're waiting for your revelation, Mr. Tripp," Borodin said. He was the one to watch, whatever happened next.

Tripp was prepared to lie his ass off in the name of self-preservation, but he didn't feel like placing a gun at his own head if he could avoid it. Ignoring Borodin for the moment, he turned to Santiago and said, "I understand you have a prisoner from Nassau."

Santiago nodded slowly. "Caught in Nassau, yes, but not Bahamian."

"Has he spilled anything so far?"

Santiago's gaze slid toward Borodin, his frown deepening. "Unfortunately, no. We are about to let Eduardo question him."

Relieved, Tripp said, "Okay, here's what I think you'll hear from him—or part of it, at least."

He'd had some forty hours to rehearse the lie, honing it to a razor's edge in places, keeping the rest of it suitably vague. His sources, Tripp claimed, were various contacts he'd managed to rattle with threats or seduce with persuasion since the Nassau blow-up. None of them held the big picture, but each provided another piece of the puzzle.

"It's an official covert operation," he began, knowing these men were well acquainted with the dirty deeds of governments around the world and the lengths to which some overzealous or corrupt police and soldiers might be driven in a pinch.

"Black ops. I couldn't pin it down much more than that. Smart money says it's Washington, but there could be a British interest in preserving Grover Halsey, too."

Way down the table, Maxwell Reed flinched at the mention of his adversary's name. Tripp was about to forge ahead, when Borodin cut in to interrupt him.

"All this from police?" he said, sounding incredulous. "No warrants, no arrests? What do they want, pray tell?"

"What do you think they want?" Tripp answered with a question of his own, then filled the gap with words before the Russian could reply. "Let's look around the table, shall we? What I see are notorious criminals, funding a guerrilla war against a fairly stable, fairly democratic government in the Caribbean. That's the game countries play, not crime Families. They want to punish you and spoil the game, but they can't do it officially without airing too much of their own dirty laundry in the process. Hence, black ops."

Borodin looked as if he didn't know whether to laugh or lunge across the table and sink his fingers into Tripp's windpipe. Tripp was ready for either, as the Russian shook his head, suddenly feigning weariness, and said, "Such daydreams. How can we believe this thing?"

Tripp gave them chapter and verse, adding some embellishments to the practiced lie as he went along, deleting other things that seemed too pat or threatened to contradict him. His audience sat and listened, different members interrupting now and then with pointed questions, Tripp fielding most of them with a frank admission of ignorance on names, dates and operational details.

When Tripp was finished, Borodin resumed his head-shaking, frowning like a disappointed uncle who's just caught his favorite nephew stealing from the cookie jar. "It's a fantastic story," Borodin said, "and I mean that sincerely. It's fantastic—a pipe dream! You've managed to stay alive this long, Mr. Tripp, but I believe you will not be the ultimate survivor."

"Before you vote me off the island," Tripp replied, "I think you ought to know I have a plan."

KENJI TANAKA WAITED until Tripp had left the room and closed the door behind him, then remarked, "I must admit, the plan makes sense to me."

Across the table, Borodin was making faces like a monkey at the zoo. "I don't believe my ears," he said. "A man of your intelligence believes that fairy tale, Tanaka-san? You trust this man who's had so many second chances I can't count them all?"

Tanaka kept his face impassive, storing up the insults for a day when retribution would be more convenient. "I don't care whether that one lives or dies," he answered Borodin. "I said the plan makes sense."

"What plan? Is that a plan?" Borodin asked, piggy eyes sweeping the table in search of support. "Tripp wants to move the prisoner—our only prisoner—to Isla de Victoria. And why? Because he thinks our enemies will follow him!"

"The evidence so far supports his theory," Santiago said. "That part of it, at least. You brought the prisoner from Nassau to Colombia, and the killing started here."

Tanaka almost smiled as Borodin smelled the trap he had set for himself. Cautiously, without the theatrical gestures, the Russian told Santiago, "It was your idea for me to bring him here. Let's not forget that, eh?"

"I have forgotten nothing," the Colombian replied, with cold steel in his voice. "No more than you, I think."

"All right," Borodin said. "Suppose Tripp's plan did work. What, then? What have we gained by setting these unknown commandos loose upon the island? How does that advance our cause? From where I sit, it seems to make the problem worse."

"Your view is clouded," Tanaka said, "by your personal dislike for Mr. Tripp. You wish him ill, and therefore do not truly listen to his plan."

"By all means then, Tanaka-san, enlighten me!"

"It is my pleasure, Comrade Borodin." Tanaka loved seeing the Russian squirm under that hated title. "Drawing the enemy to Isla de Victoria achieves three things. First, it delays further damage to our businesses, since we presently have no establishments on the island. Second, it places our adversaries at a strategic and numerical disadvantage. They'll be stepping into a war zone, badly outnumbered, with even the government troops ranged against them."

Tanaka paused, and Borodin seized on the moment. "You said three things."

"Indeed. The third, I thought, would be most obvious. Having our adversaries on the island helps our cause by casting Grover Halsey as a puppet of foreign interests. We have only to kill one or two of the intruders and arrange for their bodies to be found in government attire, with government equipment."

"Only? We have *only* to arrange this simple thing?" Borodin was red-faced with a mixture of anger and incredulity. "And how do you propose we accomplish this, Tanaka-san?"

"It should not be too difficult," the Yakuza leader replied, "since we already have one of the enemy in custody."

Tanaka sat smiling, listening while the others weighed in with comments, questions and suggestions. Through it all, Semyon Borodin remained atypically silent, whispering only once, and then briefly, to his bald Russian companion.

After several moments of disjointed back-and-forth palaver, Hector Santiago cleared his throat and raised a hand. "Gentlemen? Gentlemen, if you please." He waited for the cross-talk to subside and every eye to find his face before he spoke again. "At this time, I believe we should vote on whether to accept the new plan. All those in favor?"

Up and down the table hands were raised. From the TV sets, Sun Zu-wang and Don Ambrosio chimed in with favorable votes. When it was done, only Borodin withheld his support.

"It's carried, then," Santiago announced. He keyed the intercom at his elbow and said something in Spanish that included Tripp's name. A moment later, the door to the conference room opened again, and Tripp made his way back to his seat. Ill at ease, he did not sit this time, but remained standing beside the chair.

"So, what's the word?" Tripp asked.

"You have been fortunate today," Santiago replied. "You have one final chance to prove yourself."

Before Tripp could relax, the Russian, leaning forward, added, "And we do mean final chance. Make no mistake."

BOLAN HEARD HIS CAPTORS coming back and wondered if Eduardo would be leading the parade this time. It hardly mattered, in the long run, but a part of him wanted to delay the inevitable as long as he could, to buy more time for the others and whatever plans they had hatched since he was bagged.

The door opened behind him, footsteps circling the straight-backed wooden chair where bonds of steel and nylon held him fast.

A moment later, three men stood before him. Grim Eduardo on the left, a stranger on the right—and in the middle, Garrett Tripp.

"Nobody's introduced us yet," the mercenary said. "Name's Tripp. And you are?"

Bolan said nothing.

"Strong silent type," Tripp said. "Okay, let's run with that. Eduardo here's been hoping he can use you for his science project, just in case you didn't know. Ever have one of those anatomical models when you were a kid? The Visible Man? No skin or anything, just let it all hang out. That could be you."

Eduardo smiled. Bolan said nothing.

"I was thinking we might try a different angle of attack, though, if you don't mind staying in one piece for a while— or even if you do. I mean," Tripp added, "since your cover's already blown."

Surprised by that, Bolan shifted slightly but said nothing.

"Right, that struck a nerve," Tripp said. "Here's the thing, my man. I've figured out your deal, but knowing the other side's game plan and winning the game aren't necessarily the same thing. You follow me? Of course you do."

Bolan waited, his mind churning as he tried to guess if Tripp was bluffing, or if he really knew something—and, if so, how he had worked it out.

"We know your buddies didn't like losing you. 'No man left behind,' and all that happy crappy, right? They took the bait last night, from what I understand, but wriggled off the hook and nipped some fingers in the process."

Bolan didn't try to hide his smile.

"You like that, don't you? Hell, who wouldn't?" Tripp was smiling with him. "I'd be tickled pink if I was in your shoes, thinking my people had a plan to extricate me. But the trouble is, you see, by the time they find out where you are, you won't be here."

No smiling now.

"Don't worry, though," Tripp said. "We won't just leave them hanging. Rest assured of that. We'll leave a nice clear trail, the kind a blind man couldn't miss."

"They're not that stupid," Bolan said.

"He speaks!" Tripp cracked a thousand-candlepower smile. "Hey, that's a start. But we both know you're lying, don't we, Slick? They'd follow you to hell and back, which, as I've got it planned, is pretty much what they're about to do. Except— I'll bet you guessed it, right?—they won't be coming back."

Bolan imagined Johnny, Grimaldi and Ross surrounded, dropping in a swarm of bullets. It could still be worse, and he imagined that, as well.

"Sorry to spoil your day," Tripp lied. "I thought we'd get along better if you knew what was happening, but maybe I was wrong."

Eduardo stood, hands clasped behind his back, and smirked, enjoying it.

"You don't know what you're getting into," Bolan said.

"We'll see. My money's on the big battalions, but the good news is, you won't have to sit around watching your buddies get turned into mincemeat. Eduardo wants to tag along and keep you company. Who knew you guys would hit it off that way? I'm betting he can come up with a dozen great distractions for you, eh?"

"A hundred," Eduardo replied. "Maybe more."

"There you are," Tripp told him. "Never a dull moment."

4

Washington, D.C.

Hal Brognola took the call on his private line with a sense of foreboding. Seventy-odd percent of the calls he received on that line were bad news, and those odds had dramatically increased within the past few days. Before he even lifted the receiver, he was ready for another body blow.

"Hello?"

"It's me," Johnny Gray said. "I'm turning on the scrambler now."

"Wait one." Brognola punched a button on the base of his telephone and waited five seconds for the green light to give him a go-ahead. "Okay, we're ready. Let's hear it."

"We missed him," Johnny said, no sweetening the bitter medicine, no pulling punches. "They had airborne reinforcements waiting for us. We were suckered."

"Damn it! Are the rest of you all right?"

"We're fine, unless you judge by morale. Looks like we have to start from scratch."

"Meaning?" Brognola had a hunch, but he preferred to hear it from the kid.

"Turn up the heat on Santiago," Johnny said, as Brognola expected. "Squeeze him until he lets Mack go, or there's nobody left to take a message."

Brognola had been trying to rehearse the next bit, knowing that it wouldn't go down smoothly, if at all.

"Your brother's safety is a high priority, but it's already compromised. You may, in fact, already be too late." Brognola hated to consider the consequences.

"I don't believe that." Johnny's voice was firm.

"Forty-one hours and counting," Brognola reminded him, knowing even as he spoke that Johnny would have it calculated down to the second. "If he's alive, they've been working on him for the better part of two days."

"All the more reason to get him out soon," Johnny said.

"You know it doesn't always work that way."

"It never does, unless somebody tries."

"Your brother's one of a kind," Brognola said.

"That's why we can't afford to lose him."

"Right. But what if we already have?"

"They're using him for bait," Johnny replied.

"That doesn't mean he's still alive. It doesn't even mean he's in Colombia. They only have to make you think so, and you're on the hook."

"They missed their first pass, and they lost some people in the process."

"So, they'll be more careful next time," Brognola replied.

"They won't have the option."

"Three against the world, eh?"

"Hector Santiago's not the world. He only thinks he is."

"Down there, he's close enough," Brognola answered. "Look, just let me send somebody down to back you up, at least."

"There's no time, Hal," Johnny insisted. "I've already got the next move planned."

"Which is?"

"Kick ass, take names, leave messages. You want to help me, what I *really* need is a personal contact number for Santiago himself. No cutouts or go-betweens, no interpreters."

"I'll see what I can do. Your cell number's the same?"

"That's negative," Johnny replied. "We won't be taking any calls until we're finished here, but I'll get back to you ASAP."

Brognola tried to think of something else to say, some new appeal or angle of attack that would persuade Johnny to think twice, to be sensible. And even as the wheels were turning in his head, the big Fed knew it wouldn't work.

The Bolan brothers might be years apart in age, but in some ways they were identical. The sense of duty was hard-wired into both of them. They shared the inability to quit once battle had been joined and stubborn defiance of the most outlandish odds.

"Okay, then. I'll get onto DEA about that phone number. Meanwhile, if you need anything at all—"

"I know where to find you."

"All right."

"And Hal?"

"Uh-huh."

"Thank you."

The link was gone before he could respond—and what would he have said, in any case? Thanks for what? Thanks for nothing.

Brognola cradled the receiver, then immediately reached out for his other telephone. If nothing else, at least he could reach out and try to get a damned phone number from his man at DEA.

Medellín, Colombia

THE HOTEL ROOM FELT claustrophobic. After racing through the forest and soaring through the air like a fish on a line, four walls seemed to constrict upon Keely Ross like something from a tale by Edgar Allan Poe. Waiting for Johnny didn't help, she decided. In fact—

"He's been gone a long time," she remarked.

"Only half an hour," Grimaldi said. "It just feels long."

"You don't think he'd do something crazy on his own, do you?"

Grimaldi smiled at that. "You mean as opposed to the crazy things we do together? No, I don't think so. My guess is the man he's talking to in Washington went for the hard-sell approach and he's hit a brick wall."

"I don't follow," she told him.

"The guy we normally report to won't enjoy being cut out of the action. He'll want to send help."

"That's a *bad* thing?" Ross asked him.

"Normally, no. Any port in a storm, like they say. The more the merrier—pick your own cliché. But this is different."

"Because?"

"Johnny and Matt go back. *Way* back, okay? It's almost like a family thing."

"Okay. I picked up some of that."

"And in a case like this, two things argue against calling the cavalry. First there's time. Johnny knows every minute spent waiting for help is a minute he didn't spend trying his damnedest to wrap this thing up. He can't just sit around the hotel or the airport, killing time."

"I get that," Ross replied. "What's the second thing?"

"He doesn't trust the job to anyone else. Our friend in

Washington could send the best, even people Johnny knows, but it's still not the same. They might miss something, maybe overlook some angle Johnny wants to try."

Ross frowned. "You know the flip side, right? They could see something that he's overlooked."

"Johnny won't see it that way."

"Obviously you don't, either."

Grimaldi shrugged. "It's not my call."

"So, tell me this. What happens if we never find Matt, or we find him dead?"

Grimaldi matched her frown with one of his own. "In that case," he said, "I wouldn't want to be on Santiago's team."

"And what about the rest of it?" she asked. "This wasn't a vendetta when it started."

"Oh, don't worry," Grimaldi said. "There'll be hell enough to go around."

"That's comforting," she said, with no attempt to veil the sarcasm.

"It should be, in a way. He'd do the same for either one of us."

A sudden rapping on the door brought Grimaldi to his feet, pistol in hand. Ross stiffened, instinctively reaching for her own side arm. Grimaldi glanced at her, then nodded toward the door.

"Who is it?" she called out.

A gruff male voice came back at her.

"Police, *Señora.* Please open the door."

JOHNNY PARKED the rental car behind his hotel and spent another moment resting in the driver's seat. He checked the parking lot from force of habit, but found nothing out of place. The cars around him seemed to be unoccupied, and there was no one loitering around the garbage bins to his left.

That should have been a relief, but Johnny couldn't come close to that feeling.

Only when Mack was free and safe would he feel relieved. Unfortunately, every passing hour made a successful extraction less likely.

Brognola had been right on that score. Santiago's people could spread stories about their gringo prisoner all over Colombia, naming a hundred different hideouts, but it didn't mean Mack was alive. If he *was* still breathing, Johnny had no doubt that every hour his brother spent in captivity would be used to extract information—or to punish him for daring to challenge the cartel.

Johnny double-checked his pistol, then left the car and locked it. There was nothing in the way of furtive movement to suggest a lurking spy, nothing to place him on a higher level of alert than he already occupied. Still, Johnny listened for the sound of footsteps trailing after him as he proceeded into the hotel through a side entrance, moving toward the lobby and the bank of elevators there.

On a whim, he chose to take the stairs. The room he shared with Keely Ross was on the hotel's fourth floor, near the south end of the corridor, with Grimaldi's room just across the hall. The stairwell, on the other hand, was on the north side of the building.

Johnny saw the strangers as soon as he opened the stairwell door. There were three of them, all average size, dressed in the flashy trash that often passed for style among hoodlums. Their hair was longish and heavily oiled, combed back from dark, clean-shaven faces. The baggy cut of their jackets didn't disguise the fact they were armed. They stood outside the room he shared with Ross, their backs to Jack Grimaldi's door.

Johnny slipped back into cover, leaving the door cracked

just enough to watch them as the leader of the trio raised a hand and hammered on the door.

EMILIO RODRIGUEZ HATED working search details, but he could not refuse the order when it came down from El Jefe. Everyone, without exception, was commanded to discover new arrivals in the Medellín vicinity and check them out in detail. If suspicious characters were found, an operation would be mounted to extract them for interrogation. Failing that, elimination was the rule.

At each hotel, the routine was the same. Rodriguez and his two young soldiers braced the clerk or manager, displayed a set of more-or-less legitimate police credentials and demanded the names of any guests arriving in the past twenty-four hours.

The Casa de las Palmas had five new guests. Two were Japanese, the manager explained, some kind of businessmen from Tokyo. The other three were gringos, but one of them was female, which confused Rodriguez. Checking the registry, he found one listing for a married couple, John and Karen Grayson, and a single room for Joseph Garibaldi. Nervously, the manager assured Rodriguez that their passports were in order, and the charges to their gold credit cards had been rapidly approved.

The soldiers rode the elevator to the fourth floor in silence. Rodriguez then led the way down the hall. At the far end, flanked by doors, he had a choice to make.

"This one," Rodriguez said, after a moment's hesitation. Joseph Garibaldi was the gringo who had checked in alone, an hour after the Graysons had registered. Rodriguez thus considered him a more likely prospect for some covert action—but nobody answered his knock at the door.

One of his companions glared and asked Rodriguez, "Should I smash it?"

"No. We try the others first."

Crossing the hall, Rodriguez knocked again, aware this time of muffled conversation on the other side of the door. Five seconds passed before a woman asked, "Who is it?"

Staring at the peephole, where a moving shadow blocked the light, Rodriguez said, "Police, *Señora*. Please open the door."

"One moment, please."

Rodriguez was about to knock again when the door opened—not fully, but only to the limit of a fragile security chain. He could have bulled through it, had done so before, but the sight of the woman deterred him.

"Forgive me, Officer, but I'm not dressed."

Rodriguez saw her pale shoulder and arm were bare as the woman clutched a towel to her breast. He couldn't see the rest of her concealed behind the door, but from her face and the ripe swelling underneath the towel, Rodriguez thought she might be worth a closer look.

"Señora Grayson?"

"Yes, that's right. Is there a problem?"

"If your husband has a moment, we have certain questions."

"Questions?" There was a delicious tremor in her voice.

"Strictly routine. If we could step inside…"

"My husband isn't here," she said.

"Oh, no?" Rodriguez frowned, "but you were talking to someone, just now."

"My husband, yes."

Rodriguez blinked. "But if he isn't here—"

"He telephoned to let me know he'll be an hour late. He's in a business meeting with the first vice president of Banco de Medellín. We're going out to dinner afterward. That's why…" She blushed and gripped the towel more tightly, edging farther out of sight behind the door.

Rodriquez knew El Jefe did business with Banco de Medellín. There would be trouble if Rodriguez made a scene and angered the vice president.

Rodriguez compromised. "Perhaps another time," he said. "*Señora*, please forgive the interruption."

"Not at all," she answered, visibly relieved. "I'll tell my husband to expect your visit."

"*Gracias.*"

A real detective would have handed the woman a business card, but Rodriguez, watching raptly as the towel slipped from her breast, had only the badge to bolster his charade.

The door closed as he turned away and moved back toward the elevator, with the youngsters trailing him. "That's all?" one of them asked. "You take her word?"

"Did you mistake her for a soldier, *stupido*?" Rodriguez snarled. "We'll come back for the other one tonight, and maybe see the Graysons afterward. Right now, we still have nine hotels to check."

GRIMALDI WAITED, gun in hand, and watched Ross scan the outer hallway through the peephole in the door. He had a decent view of the lady's topless profile. The towel was gripped in her right hand, while she held a pistol in her left.

"I think they're gone," Ross told him, not quite whispering. She moved back toward the bed, where her blouse and brassiere lay tangled together. "Sorry for flashing you there. It was all I could think of."

"I wasn't complaining," Grimaldi assured her.

"Okay. You can turn around now."

"In the interest of security—"

"Just do it!"

He did it. Standing easy with the Beretta while fabric rustled behind him. "Did they look like cops?" he asked.

"Who knows, down here? Three of them, on a routine call? Now that you mention it, I thought their hair was on the shaggy side."

"Something to think about," Grimaldi said.

"Okay, I'm decent."

"That makes one of us." He turned, slipping the autoloader back into its holster.

"Do you think they have this place staked out?" Ross asked.

"No way to tell without a recon."

"Johnny!" Ross had just sat down, and now she bounded to her feet again.

Grimaldi didn't need to ask her what she meant. If the police—or someone else—had the hotel under surveillance, checking out the gringo new arrivals, Johnny would be an easy mark when he returned.

The cell phone chirped as Grimaldi was reaching for it. Surprised, he flipped it open, raised it to his ear and said, "Hello?"

"I saw the welcoming committee split," Johnny announced. "Did they leave anything behind?"

"Not that I know of," the pilot replied, flashing a thumbs-up sign to Ross. "Of course, we haven't checked outside."

"The hallway's clear as far as I can tell."

"Where are you?"

"Coming off the service stairs on four right now. Give me one-twenty, if there's no surprise along the way."

"Affirmative."

Grimaldi closed and pocketed the telephone, while counting off 120 seconds in his mind. "He's back."

"Where?" Ross asked.

"The far end of the hallway, homing in."

Impulsively, she started for the door.

"I wouldn't do that," Grimaldi warned.

She stood her ground, waiting, until a key turned in the lock. Grimaldi had his pistol drawn again, but stowed it as Johnny entered, closing the door behind him.

"Clear on this floor, anyway," Johnny said.

"You want to risk it?" Grimaldi asked.

"Staying?" Johnny shook his head. "Forget it. We've got things to do and time is running short. We may as well clear out."

"I'm glad I never really got unpacked," Ross said. "Give me five minutes?"

"Five it is," Johnny replied.

"I'll get my stuff and meet you in the hall," Grimaldi said.

Johnny stood by to cover him as he stepped out into the hallway.

It was still clear. Grimaldi used the plastic key card and let himself into the room across the hall. The word from Washington could wait until they reached the car and put the compromised hotel behind them, going—where?

Johnny had mentioned having things to do, and if experience had taught him anything, Grimaldi knew the younger Bolan hadn't planned a picnic or a shopping spree. Whatever he had learned—or hadn't learned—from Brognola, the kid had come back galvanized for action.

It's going to be a hot time in the old town tonight, Grimaldi thought. He only hoped they weren't the ones who wound up getting burned.

"I WAS AFRAID THEY'D pick you off outside," Ross said. She'd stepped into his arms as soon as Grimaldi had left the room, but Johnny held her only long enough for one quick kiss.

"They may be waiting when we hit the parking lot," he told her. "Either way, we're running short on time."

They spent the next three minutes stuffing toiletries and clothing into duffel bags. Their weapons were already packed, but still accessible if they were ambushed on their way down to the street.

Unless the ambush took them down without warning.

"Ready!" Ross held two bags in her left hand, dragging down her shoulder on that side, but it left her gun hand free. Johnny followed her example, gave the room a final scan and led the way outside.

Grimaldi met them in the corridor, right hand inside his jacket as he said, "All clear, so far."

"Let's hope it stays that way," Johnny replied.

They moved single file along the corridor, Johnny leading, Ross behind him and Grimaldi bringing up the rear. They met no one along the way and heard nothing from the rooms they passed. The dead hour of the afternoon, between work and playtime, gave them a clear path to the service stairs.

No one even suggested the elevator. It would take them to the lobby, and if anyone was watching for them that would be the prime location for a spotter. There might still be others on the street or in the parking lot, but Johnny saw no reason to begin their flight betting heavily against the odds.

They took it slow and easy on the stairs, making as little noise as possible, no talking, hands on hidden pistols all the way. At every landing, Johnny stopped and listened, straining to detect the slightest sound of watchers down below: a whispered word, a shoe sole scuffing concrete, anything.

Nothing.

They retreated and made their way toward a service entrance at the rear. Johnny walked a little faster than on the stairs, less careful of the noise as he proceeded. Only one door stood between them and the parking lot, their car, the open road.

The last door had a window set at eye level, wire mesh sandwiched by two panes of glass. Johnny sidestepped and craned his neck to have a cautious look outside, scanning the sidewalk and the hotel parking lot as far as he was able.

"Looks clear," he said. "Stay frosty, though."

The service stairs and corridor were not cooled by the hotel's air-conditioning, but still the outer heat slapped Johnny in the face like a wet rag as he stepped through the doorway into sunshine and humidity no native of the Northern Hemisphere would ever truly understand.

He half expected gunmen to come springing from the trash bins, trailing garbage in their wake, but none appeared. A solitary raven hopped about between the cars, searching for scraps of food. Johnny ignored it, since the black bird wasn't packing heat, and moved on to the rental car.

When they were finally rolling and clean, without a tail, Grimaldi asked from the back seat, "What's the word from Wonderland?"

"They want to send the cavalry. I told them to forget it." Johnny sounded grim.

Wary silence hung heavy in the car. Johnny knew what they were thinking. He had already walked that mental ground himself and recognized the pitfalls. Most of them were fatal.

"So, what's the drill?" Grimaldi eventually asked.

"We've got two ways to go," Johnny replied. "One way is kicking ass until somebody squeals."

"And what's the other way?" Ross asked from the shotgun seat.

"Dig up another source and try to find out where they're holding Matt."

"Can we do that?"

"It may mean working up the food chain, if we've got the time."

Time was the enemy, he knew. Each hour made it that much more unlikely that he'd ever see his brother in the living flesh again.

"Plan B sounds like it has a better chance of working out," Ross said.

"I'll second that," Grimaldi added from the rear.

"Okay," Johnny replied. "Let's try it on for size."

Plan A would still be waiting if they needed it, a scorched-earth fallback option with a one-way ticket to the Land of No Return.

"Where do we start?" Ross asked him.

"In the gutter," Johnny said. "Where else?"

5

Serrania de Macarena, Colombia

"It's only for a short time, I assure you."

Semyon Borodin nodded, but he could not resist a smile. "I understand, Hector, of course. I simply never thought I'd see the day when you were forced to run and hide within your own country."

"We all hide," Santiago answered stiffly. "Every day we hide our assets, our intentions, our alliances. Surely, you won't pretend things are so different in Russia that you carry out your business in the open light of day."

"My business, no," Borodin conceded. "But when I punish my enemies, I turn a spotlight on them for the education of whoever else may try to follow in their footsteps."

They were traveling along a narrow, winding mountain road, their vehicle the third of six in a line. Their destination was a "home away from home," as Santiago called it, which he promised was impervious to outside threats. After four hours on the road, Borodin was wishing they could at least stop and take a break.

"I've made examples in my time, some recently. You know

it's true," the Colombian said. "You *also* know that our collaborative effort must not be revealed until we have secured the victory. It will be risky, even then, but any premature exposure could be disastrous."

"I understand that," Borodin replied, "but if Tripp's story is correct, then the Americans *already* know, and they're committed to destroying us. What is the point of hiding what we call an open war?"

"It is our nature, Semyon. Don't you know that yet? We're creatures of the shadows, night dwellers. Those of us who court publicity, from Capone in Chicago to Noriega in Panama City, bring disaster upon themselves. You must know this by now. You're not a child."

Borodin bit off the acid response that came swiftly to mind. In its place, he replied, "I have invested millions in a sanctuary where my interests will be served. It is ridiculous to say that I must now pretend to be ashamed."

"It's curious that you equate caution with shame. I hope that's not a fatal flaw—for your sake."

Borodin stared hard at Santiago's craggy face, wondering if he should take the remark as a threat, but he convinced himself to let it go—for now. The vehicle in front of them was slowing, forcing the others in the convoy to do likewise. Borodin craned forward, striving for a view of something, anything that would suggest they'd reached their destination. But the tinted windows showed him only trees and boulders.

"Just another thirty minutes," Santiago reassured him. "More or less."

"You have electric power there and running water?" Borodin inquired.

"We have all the amenities, and some which you might not expect. As I told you before, this is my home away from home."

"And if our enemies should find us here? Then, what?"

"They won't. By now, they're nibbling at our bait and opening their jaws to take the hook."

"Let's hope so," Borodin replied.

But if you're wrong, he thought, as they began to climb a one-lane track in four-wheel drive, we're trapped here. We're as good as dead.

Downtown Medellín

"YOU THINK THEY'LL BE open for business tonight?" Jack Grimaldi asked.

"Business never stops," Johnny answered. "It's what they live for."

"But the brass—"

"We don't need brass," Johnny said. "All we need is someone in the know."

"I'm wondering," Ross interjected, "why you don't think they'll bait another trap."

"I'm sure they will," Johnny stated.

"But, then—"

"They'll bait a trap, all right," Johnny continued, "but this time, they'll have the bait on hand to make it work. We beat them in the first round. They took heavy losses. We've been whipping them for days. They want this over with as bad as we do. Maybe more."

"Okay," she said, "granting all that, I still don't see what makes you think Matt's still alive."

Grimaldi watched and waited in the back seat, weighing the kid's reaction, studying his eyes in the rental's rearview mirror.

"Because they still need him," Johnny responded. "First, they wanted information. Now, he's their only link to the rest of the team. Santiago knows he has to suck us in before he can destroy us."

"And we're helping him?" Ross asked.

"Not quite. Last time, the trap was empty and it failed. They won't take any chances on the second round."

"Where do you think they'll take him?"

Johnny considered it, then shook his head. "If I knew that, we could eliminate the middleman."

"We'll have to do that anyway," Grimaldi said, "unless you plan on picking up a native guide."

"No, thanks," Johnny said. "Information is all we're after."

"And you think we'll find it at this place we're going?" Grimaldi asked.

"It's a starting point."

"What do they call the place again?" Ross asked.

"El Deguello," Johnny said.

Grimaldi smiled. "That's classic."

"Why?" Ross half turned in her seat to face him.

"It's the name of a tune," Grimaldi told her. "Mexican generals used to have their buglers play it on the eve of battle, when they planned to show no mercy. Santa Anna played it at the Alamo."

"Is that supposed to be encouraging?"

Grimaldi let her see another smile. "It's just a footnote. One thing might improve your humor, though."

"Oh, yeah? What's that?"

"This time, the bad guys are playing defense."

Ross frowned. "It didn't seem that way, at the hotel."

"They're looking, but they missed again. That little striptease did the trick."

Ross blushed, as Johnny glanced her way and asked, "What's this?"

"I had to throw them off, okay? Forget about it."

"That's a tall order," Grimaldi said. "You could get an Oscar nod for that kind of well-rounded performance."

Johnny was laughing now for the first time since the mission started. Ross joined him a moment later, while Grimaldi sat back and watched the neon scenery sliding past his window.

Simply cruising up and down the streets of Medellín, no one would guess it was the heart of an illicit empire based on misery and death. The casual observer wouldn't know that Colombia ranked first or second among Western nations for per capita murders each year. The unenlightened tourist wouldn't know which strangers passing on the street owed their survival to the cocaine trade and the corruption it had spawned.

The city's mask was more or less intact, but Johnny meant to shatter it, and Grimaldi was going along for the ride. He'd signed on willingly, even enthusiastically, and nothing that had happened in the interim had changed his mind.

"We're almost there," Johnny said. "The next block, I think. If I could see the numbers—there it is!"

Grimaldi studied El Deguello as they motored past it, headed east with the flow of traffic. For a nightclub, it appeared sedate. There was no line outside, no partygoers milling on the sidewalk, nothing to suggest the building's inner life except its name. That was emblazoned on a jet-black wall in crimson neon, like a message painted in fresh blood.

No quarter asked or offered here, it seemed to say.

Okay, Grimaldi thought, as Johnny drove around the block. At least I know the rules.

RICARDO CIGLIANO LIT a cigarette, drew deeply on it once, then stubbed it out in a crystal ashtray. He was trying to cut back on smoking, but at the moment there was simply too much tension in his life to quit cold turkey.

Tension? Make that paranoid anxiety.

Cigliano knew what had happened to Pablo Aznar in Nassau, and he'd heard enough details of the recent bloody business in the mountains to know they were at war. That wasn't so unusual, guerrilla warfare being more or less the normal state of life in the cocaine industry, but this time no one seemed to know who they were fighting.

Or, rather, no one had bothered to tell *him*.

Being kept in the dark was one thing, but what Cigliano truly resented was being used as a pawn. He didn't get that feeling often, having worked his way up through the ranks of the Santiago organization to a post in solid middle management, but today was an exception.

All because of the phone call.

Pablo Aznar's replacement, Ramon Montoya, had placed the call himself. The message had been brief and anything but clear. If someone asks you, Cigliano had been told, say that the hostage has been moved to Isla de Victoria.

What hostage? *Never mind.*

Who would be asking? *We're not sure.*

What if they don't believe me? *Use your own initiative.*

Cigliano couldn't tell Montoya what he longed to say, not without putting his own neck on the chopping block, so now he sat in his office at El Deguello and sneaked cigarettes like a schoolboy hiding in the bathroom, waiting for some unknown calamity to strike.

From what Montoya didn't say, Cigliano thought he could piece together some of the puzzle. The cartel was at war with someone from outside, a force large and strong enough to strike in Nassau and outside of Medellín while evading retaliation. Still, they'd made a slip of some sort, letting one of their own be captured by El Jefe's soldiers. Montoya expected others to come looking for the prisoner, and he was giving them directions—why?

To bait a trap, why else?

The scheme was so transparent that Cigliano couldn't believe anyone would fall for it. Unless, of course, the information was true.

Why would the enemy ask him? How would they even know that Ricardo Cigliano existed?

Again, he knew the answer, more or less. This enemy had studied Santiago's operation in detail before attacking, worked out targets in advance and run profiles on personnel. That told Cigliano that the enemy was either an official agency or a rival cartel on par with El Jefe's. In either case, it was bad news for those caught in the middle.

In El Jefe's organization, Cigliano was expendable, and no one knew it better than himself.

Which explained his selection to be a messenger boy.

Had Montoya done something to single him out? Was the greasy little bastard spotlighting Cigliano in some way, to make the enemy focus on him? It seemed preposterous, unthinkable. And yet—

Cigliano was reaching for another cigarette when he decided it was time to leave. El Deguello could survive without him until closing time. His assistant manager craved an opportunity to show his mettle, and this would be a start. Cigliano would go home, relax and forget about answering questions for strangers with guns in their hands.

Ten minutes later, after spitting orders at his startled subordinate, Cigliano left the club through a private rear exit and walked to his car. It was a black Mercedes-Benz, the closest thing he had to a badge of rank in the cartel.

Cigliano had deactivated the alarm, unlocked the door, and he was reaching for the handle when a scuffling sound behind him made him hesitate. He had begun to turn, when something struck his skull with numbing force and he was slumped into darkness without end.

JOHNNY CAUGHT THE MAN as he was falling, knees flexed to support the weight. He'd used enough force to induce unconsciousness without inflicting lethal damage—or, at least, he hoped so.

"Anyone we know?" Grimaldi asked, as he stepped forward to shoulder a share of the burden.

"Never saw him before in my life," Johnny said. "He just came out the door marked Private and I saw him headed for the Benz. He's not your average button man."

Ross had the trunk lid open when they reached the rental car. Johnny and Grimaldi supported the slack form of their captive while Ross used a roll of duct tape to secure his wrists, then knelt to do the ankles. Finally, racing the clock, she wrapped a twist around his lower face, sealing his lips. That done, they tucked him out of sight in the trunk, closed it and got back in the car.

"We need someplace to take him," Grimaldi said.

"I was thinking of a nice ride in the country," Johnny answered. "We can pick a spot outside of town and go off-road."

"What if he doesn't have the answers?" Ross inquired.

"If at first you don't succeed," Johnny replied.

"Try, try again," she finished for him. "Right. I get it."

"If you have a better idea…"

"I might not have been so quick to reject the assistance."

"We've been over that," Johnny said. "By the time they get here—"

"We could all be dead," Ross interrupted. "I've considered it, believe me. The way we're going, it's not that unlikely."

"You can still get out," Johnny replied. "Just tell me where to drop you off."

She fixed him with a glare, one eyebrow cocked for maximum effect. From where Grimaldi sat, he couldn't tell if Ross was angry, surprised, or some volatile combination of both.

"Bail out and leave the two of you down here alone to make a mess of things? I don't think so. Just drive the car and leave the jokes to someone with a sense of humor, okay?" Ross snarled.

Grimaldi gave her points for nerve and felt himself relax a notch when Johnny smiled. They were light-years away from safe, but any kind of simmering disharmony within the team would only make things worse, boosting the odds that none of them would come out on the other side alive.

His thoughts returned to Mack, and what the Executioner had to be going through. It didn't help to dwell on details, but Grimaldi had the gist of it. He'd never personally suffered through interrogation or the kind of torture that's inspired by fury and frustration, but Grimaldi knew the various techniques. When he was flying for the Mob, back in the days before he'd met Bolan and turned his life around, Grimaldi had provided transportation for a couple of the "doctors" who were kept on staff for special operations in the field. He knew about their gruesome tricks by word of mouth, but didn't like to dwell on it.

Someday, Grimaldi hoped, he might stockpile enough good deeds to wipe that particular stain from his soul.

And if not, at least he could go down swinging.

Johnny took it easy, heading out of town. They weren't

wanted for anything, so far, and he kept it that way, driving just above the posted speed limit to keep from stalling traffic and attracting unwelcome attention. They watched for tails along the way and found none, as expected. They were still faceless, nameless, unknown to the enemy.

Unless Mack was spilling his guts.

That image turned Grimaldi's stomach, and he pushed it brusquely out of mind. He had to believe they weren't too late, or else the whole thing became a grand exercise in futility. They'd be better off pushing to finish the mission, without this sideshow.

But he knew Johnny wouldn't abandon his brother. Not now, not ever.

Not while any shred of hope remained.

Glancing back at his window, Grimaldi saw they were out of the city and driving past dark, open fields. Five minutes later, Johnny pulled onto a narrow access road and drove until the lights of traffic passing on the distant highway looked like fireflies in the night.

He parked and killed the engine then, and half turning in his seat said, "Let's do it."

RICARDO CIGLIANO reckoned he was dead. Not literally, maybe, but the next best thing. He'd worked for Hector Santiago long enough to understand that no one—no one—drove a person out into the countryside at night to wish them well. The victims typically came back in body bags, a handful of them still alive but having suffered such atrocities they found no cause for celebrating life.

Cigliano had regained consciousness somewhere in the midst of his dark, suffocating ride to nowhere. He had no idea how long he'd been on the road and didn't suppose it mattered. The fact that he was breathing and hadn't simply been shot in the parking lot behind El Deguello might have been encouraging, except for the stories he'd heard about kidnap victims who were tortured and maimed.

It wouldn't be a ransom snatch, that much he knew for certain. Petty criminals would know he served El Jefe and would fear the wrath of his employer, while a rival narcotrafficker would realize that Cigliano was expendable. No ransom, then, and that told him his kidnappers were after information.

Suddenly, he heard Montoya's voice again. *If someone asks you, say the hostage has been moved to Isla de Victoria.*

Cigliano cursed Montoya, wondering if he'd been set up specifically for this torment, or if everyone on El Jefe's payroll had received the same briefing, Montoya covering his bets in the knowledge that someone, somewhere, would be kidnapped. It hardly mattered, either way, since Cigliano's number had come up and he was out of luck.

The car was slowing, coasting to a stop. His mind began to race, plotting what he should say when they untaped his mouth, how he should try to sell the story and to save himself.

The quickest way, of course, would be to blurt out the answer before they asked the question. He could do it that way, even as they peeled the duct tape from his burning lips, cry out, "The hostage has been moved to Isla de Victoria."

No good.

The spill-it-all-right-now approach was faulty. First, they'd be suspicious if he blurted out the information instantly, before they even asked. His kidnappers would think it was a trick—which, Cigliano thought, it obviously was. Conversely, if they did believe him, his spontaneous confession only served to make him look guilty, casting him as a principal in an incident of which he had no knowledge.

And what would they do to him then?

Cigliano shuddered to think of it, almost missing the moment when the car stopped dead and its engine was switched off. He heard the doors slam, though, and dirt or gravel crunching under shoes as his captors came to fetch him.

Cigliano closed his eyes and kept them shut as someone unlocked the trunk lid, raised it and shone a flashlight beam onto his face. They had to have seen his eyelids twitching, for a male voice said, "He's faking it."

"Come on, amigo," another man said. "It's time to rise and shine."

Cigliano opened his eyes, blinking painfully in the flashlight's glare until it swept away from his face. He was still seeing spots when hands reached into the trunk and pulled him out, manhandling him until he was upright, standing on his own two feet.

They released him, and he tried to hold the pose, but he was dizzy and his ankles were still taped together. With a muffled cry of panic, Cigliano toppled forward and collapsed onto his face.

"You think he's broken?" Grimaldi asked.

"Turn him over and find out," Johnny replied.

The man had scuffed his forehead when he fell, and blood was seeping from his nose. From where she stood, Ross couldn't tell if it was broken, and she guessed it didn't really matter. On the other hand, if it was blocked and they left duct tape on his mouth...

The prisoner was twitching, making little panic noises from behind his silver gag. "I don't think he can breathe," Ross said. "If anybody cares."

The duct tape made a ripping sound as Johnny pulled it free. The prisoner sucked wind as if he'd just emerged from swimming underwater, at the limits of endurance. Ross's estimation of him rose a notch when he kept quiet, otherwise. No questions, no pathetic pleas for mercy.

Johnny saw it, too, and leaned in closer as he said, "Do you know who we are?"

The captive shook his head, snuffling through blood.

"No thoughts at all? Nothing you've heard, the past two days or so, that clues you in on why you've been invited to this little party?"

"No."

Johnny glanced up at Ross and Grimaldi, shrugging. "Okay," he said. "I'll have to fill you in. We've been kicking your boss's ass for a while, but he got lucky, day before yesterday. He snatched one of our friends in Nassau and brought him back here. We mean to have him back, regardless of the cost. Ring any bells?"

The hostage was thinking about it. Ross could tell that from the way his face contorted. He resembled a child caught with his hand in the cookie jar, trying to decide if he'd benefit from flat-out denial, or if a tearful confession would spare him a whipping.

"He knows something," she said.

The man found her with his eyes not quite pleading, but close.

"I only know what I was told!" he blurted out.

"That may be good enough," Johnny replied. "Let's hear it."

He hesitated, then spit it out as if by rote. "The hostage has been moved to Isla de Victoria!"

Johnny relaxed his grip. "Back up," he said. "Who told you that?"

The guy blinked twice, then said, "Montoya."

Ross couldn't help herself. "You mean Ramon Montoya?"

"*Sí!*"

"When did this come down?" Johnny asked.

"Today. This afternoon. A little after two o'clock, I think."

"What else was said?" Johnny demanded.

"There is no more," the prisoner said earnestly. "Montoya says, 'If anybody asks, you tell them this.' Now you have asked, and I have answered."

"It's another setup," Grimaldi said.

Johnny nodded. "Probably."

"Try absolutely," Ross said.

"I grant you it's a trap," Johnny replied. "That doesn't mean they're lying."

Ross was confused. "Come again?"

"I mean, it could be true," Johnny said. "They want us out of here, no argument. Why not use bait?"

"Or, they could drop him in a hole," Grimaldi said, "and tell us he's been moved. It has the same effect if we fall for the story."

"Absolutely right," Johnny said, strangely calm. "I can't prove you're mistaken, but I *feel* it. This is something Santiago and the rest of them would do. It suits their temperament."

"I still don't follow you," Ross said.

"They're fighting a war on the island, right?" Johnny said. "Where better to dispose of three or four pains in the ass?"

"Why not here?" she challenged him. "They've never been shy about killing in their own backyard before."

"Not shy," Johnny said. "Worried. We've been doing all the killing up to now. Their local scam blew up in their faces and cost them plenty. It makes sense they'd want the next game to be played out of town."

"So, that's it?" Grimaldi asked.

"Not quite." Johnny drew his Beretta and aimed it at the captive's bloody face. "Sorry, amigo, but we don't need any witnesses right now."

Ross closed her eyes and waited for the shot.

Washington, D.C.

"YOU'RE SURE ABOUT THIS?" Hal Brognola asked his caller.

"No," Johnny replied, "but it feels right."

"Feels like a trap," Brognola said.

"We're counting on it, but that doesn't mean it has to go their way."

The kid was sounding like his brother, more and more. Brognola didn't want to think about one generation passing and another moving up, but it was inescapable under the circumstances.

"What's the plan?" Brognola asked, as much to stop his train of thought as to elicit information.

"As it stands right now, we're going for it. Not the way they hoped, with some kind of bull-in-a-china-shop deal, but cautiously."

"You're talking covert entry?"

"Has to be," Johnny replied. "We can't risk going through the immigration screen, with Reed's people looking over someone's shoulder. Jack can get us in, then fall back to Grenada or Antigua, somewhere close enough to catch an SOS."

Brognola didn't like the sound of that. "It's just the two of you?" he asked.

"For now."

He knew what Johnny meant by that. For now, as in, until they found his brother. Except that could turn out to be a fantasy, or they could find him dead. A hundred different things could go wrong with the plan, and Johnny didn't seem to take them seriously.

"Dropping one-third of your force isn't the best idea I've heard today," Brognola said.

"Jack's strength is in the air," Johnny reminded him. "The

other way, we paddle in together, ditch the boat and maybe find ourselves with no way off the island."

"It's your call." Brognola felt soul-weary, suddenly, as if the past two weeks were catching up to him in one big rush.

"You think I'm wrong," Johnny said. It didn't come out sounding like a question.

"Don't ask me. I've never had to make a call like this," Brognola replied. And he was hoping that he never would.

"We'd likely have to do the island anyway," Johnny said. "When you boil it down, that's where the action is. If Reed wins over Halsey, even if we take out the cartel, he'll find somebody else to grease the wheels before you turn around."

That much was true. In just two weeks, they'd gone from looking into motives for a murder to obstructing a cartel of global predators bankrolling revolution on a scenic speck in the Caribbean. They'd reached a point, in fact, where they could take out all the major heavies and yet fail, if they allowed the revolution to proceed.

Johnny was right. Nature abhorred a vacuum. If they wiped out Maxwell Reed's supporters, a new team would replace the old before the ink dried on the last stack of death certificates.

"I'd offer help," Brognola said, "but we both know how that tune goes."

"In fact," Johnny replied, "there's something you can do for me."

"Name it."

"Those other guys you talked about," Johnny went on, "have them on standby, just in case we blow it. The stakes have gone too high to let it rest if I turn out to be as big an asshole as you think I am."

"That's not the way it is," Brognola told him.

"No?"

"I thought you were too close to this, and that's still true. It doesn't mean you had a choice. Your brother never would've walked away. We both know that."

"But I'm not him."

"Who is? We'll never see his like again."

"He's not done yet. Believe it," Johnny said.

"I'm hanging in," Brognola promised. "But whichever way it goes, I've got your back. Make sure the flyboy knows that, will you?"

"Absolutely. Thanks."

Brognola nodded once, then realized his caller couldn't see it. "Right," he said. "Stay frosty, guy."

"You know it."

When the line went dead this time, Brognola sat and held the telephone receiver for a long, grim moment, listening to the dial tone. And when he set it back into its cradle, the soft click reminded him of fastening the latches on a coffin's lid.

6

Fort-de-France, Martinique

"How long?" Johnny asked, when Grimaldi passed him for the second time.

"Ten minutes, maybe fifteen," Grimaldi replied. "If it isn't right, we don't go up."

So, get it right, he thought, but kept the biting comment to himself. There was an outside chance that if Johnny pushed too hard, too far, Grimaldi would refuse to fly.

They'd chosen Martinique as the departure point because it put them slightly closer to Isla de Victoria than an airstrip on Grenada or Dominica would have done. It was supposed to be a simple out-and-back sightseeing tour, nothing to trouble anybody in the tower. There had been no questions asked about their cargo or the passengers aboard, no head count that would turn around and bite Grimaldi on the ass when he came back alone. As far as anybody knew—or cared—it was another routine day in paradise.

But Johnny wasn't interested in paradise. He had a date to keep in hell, located thirty-seven miles southeast of where he stood.

The Learjet Longhorn had conveyed them from Colombia to Martinique in just under two hours, from takeoff to touchdown. That was good time, speeding above the clouds at speeds in excess of 520 miles per hour, but Johnny still begrudged the delay, still felt as if he had been slogging through molasses every moment since his brother was captured and carried away.

It's not my fault, he kept telling himself, but the message wouldn't stick. It wasn't his fault that Mack had been taken, but Johnny had so far done nothing toward getting him back except chase false leads down blind alleys. It was humbling and infuriating. It had put him in his place—and that was not a place he cared to be.

Third time's the charm, he told himself, and hoped it was the truth. One thing was certain, anyway: If this attempt to find his brother failed, there wouldn't be another—not with Johnny at the helm, that is. This time was go-for-broke, a clear case of do-or-die.

The Learjet wasn't built for jumping, and they'd lost another ninety precious minutes on the ground at Fort-de-France, while Grimaldi went looking for an aircraft that would meet their needs. He settled for a Beech Queen Air, a low-wing twin-engine plane whose top speed was 230 miles per hour. It looked like an antique beside the Learjet, and it probably was, but Grimaldi's stamp of approval was good enough for Johnny.

Above all else, he wanted to be in the air and on his way. Whatever happened next, he needed to be doing something.

The gear was all aboard. They had four parachutes, two standard high-altitude, low opening packs—HALO—and two emergency chutes, just in case. Keely Ross had never jumped before, but she had nerve enough to try it, trusting Johnny and her wrist altimeter to tell her when the rip cord should be pulled.

Their jumpsuits were tiger-striped cammo, a touch Grimaldi had devised to cut down on excess baggage. Aside from lightweight helmets, gloves and goggles, the remainder of the weight they would be carrying was combat and survival gear: the CAR-15s, Berettas, ammunition, frag grenades and Ka-Bar knives, canteens of water, first-aid kits, and three days' worth of the standard-issue Meals, Ready to Eat—MREs—that had replaced C-rations in the U.S. military. For communication, they were carrying their two-way headsets, and Johnny was packing a compact shortwave set with a range of five hundred miles. That was roughly ten times the distance that would lie between himself and Jack Grimaldi once they hit the silk for Isla de Victoria, but he wasn't taking any chances.

"We're set," Grimaldi told him. "Are we gonna do this thing, or what?"

"I'm there," Johnny replied. He boarded ahead of Grimaldi and found Ross already belted into her seat. Grimaldi handed them oxygen bottles with floppy masks attached and took them through the drill of clipping the bottles to their jumpsuits, making sure they knew how to fasten the masks properly.

"You'll be jumping around ten thousand feet," he reminded them both. "Without the oxygen you'll lose consciousness before it's time to pull the pin, and then it's bright raspberry pancake time. Okay? So get it right the first time, if it's not too much to ask."

With that, Grimaldi took his place in the cockpit, while Johnny buckled up. There were two planes in line ahead of them for takeoff, and Johnny sat restlessly while Grimaldi taxied into position, waiting for his signal from the tower. When it came, their plane seemed to bolt down the runway, like a racehorse coming out of the gate. It was a rough ride, compared to the Learjet, but exhilarating nonetheless as they lifted off and climbed into the clouds.

"Better get cracking," Grimaldi called to them, with the plane still climbing toward its cruising altitude. "These puddle jumps don't take much time."

Calm for the first time in forty-eight hours, Johnny unfastened his seat belt and reached for his gear.

WHEN THEY REACHED ten thousand feet, Grimaldi leveled off and set a southeasterly course that would take them directly over Isla de Victoria, the pint-sized war zone that had been the focus of their efforts from the start. Down there, concealed beneath a filmy layer of clouds, men were fighting and dying for control of an island roughly half the size of the state of Delaware. At stake was control over a sovereign land, albeit tiny, that could turn crooks into kings and place them on a pedestal beyond reach of the law. It was a bold move, nervy, and Grimaldi wasn't sure they could prevent it with the time and manpower available.

But they could try.

And if his comrades failed, what then?

Grimaldi wasn't sure. He couldn't very well take off and strafe the presidential palace or rain bombs at random on the island. He'd reach out to Hal Brognola and the team at Stony Man if Johnny missed his self-imposed deadline, and after that it would be yet another game of hurry up and wait. It would be out of his hands, and Grimaldi would be fortunate if he was cast in a supporting role.

Again.

There was a certain irony to that, he realized. Technology had come a long way since the last great war, when air support was mostly that—a means of backing up the infantry and armor with a well-placed rocket, bomb or strafing run. Modern wars were fought primarily by pilots, or by technicians far removed from the scene who used "smart" weapons to do their killing for them, keeping their hands squeaky-clean. In Grimaldi's world, though, he was still air support, sidelined from involvement in the main event.

He checked his instruments and saw that they were almost on target. Four minutes and twenty-three seconds to go.

"Get ready!" he called from the cockpit. "Four minutes to step-off!"

"We're set," Johnny answered before he clamped his oxygen mask into place. Grimaldi felt the plane shudder when one of his passengers opened the door in preparation for the leap.

It was the one flaw in their plan, that door. He'd have to put the plane on automatic pilot after Ross and Johnny jumped, go back and close the door himself, to ward off any questions when he landed. There was nothing to it, really, but he didn't like to think about the short flight back to Fort-de-France, because he would be making it alone.

The stakes were the same as always. One slip, one error, and somebody died. Grimaldi had a sense that he was running out of friends. It made him wonder what he'd do when none of them were left.

"One minute!" he called, alerting them, knowing they couldn't answer. He started counting down the seconds, holding the aircraft as steady as he could.

At twenty, there was turbulence, but not enough to matter. By the time he'd counted down to ten, the air was smooth again. On one, Grimaldi held his breath and listened for some sound behind him, dreading anything that might go wrong. A moment later, when he glanced through the cabin, he was all alone.

"Good luck," he whispered. "Give 'em hell."

Ross HADN'T KNOWN that it would be this frightening. She'd jumped with her eyes closed, but she couldn't keep them shut the whole way down. She'd opened up in time to see a cloud bank rushing up at her, God only knew how fast. It felt as if she were riding a rocket sled into a fog bank, with no idea what lay on the other side.

What if they had miscalculated the altitude, somehow? What if she burst through the clouds to find jagged mountain peaks below, reaching up to smash her bones and shred her flesh? Suppose there wasn't time to pull the rip cord and she hit the stone face like a paintball splattered on the side of a garage?

To prevent her mind and body from locking up in fear, she concentrated on mechanics. Breathing was first, the oxygen ice-cold in her nostrils and throat from the bottle clipped onto her harness. Ross refused to think about what would become of her if it tore loose and blew away, or if the tank didn't contain enough to get her safely through the jump.

After the breathing, Ross focused on posture, making sure her arms and legs were held in the proper position, rigid despite the hurricane rush of wind past her body that whipped at her clothing and threatened to make her start tumbling head over heels.

You can do this, she thought, and wished she believed it.

Where's Johnny? she thought, worried.

He jumped behind her, making sure she didn't chicken out, and there was no way to spot him now that they were in the soup. She wondered if he could have passed her, his greater weight increasing velocity, and then her mind coughed up an image of Johnny hurtling down upon her from behind, smashing into her back, both of them stunned and tumbling unconscious to their deaths.

Stop that!

He'd done this kind of thing before, even if she hadn't, and he'd know enough to avoid catastrophic midair collisions.

All Ross had to think about now was the altimeter strapped to her left wrist and the rip cord handle dangling above her left breast. Ross knew reaching for the cord would throw her off balance, but by that time she'd be close enough to touch-down that it shouldn't matter. She would simply give a yank and wait for the jerk as her chute blossomed overhead, slowing her descent as if she'd slammed on a set of air brakes.

Unless the chute was faulty. In that case, she would have to quell her panic and pull the second rip cord—this one roughly on a level with her solar plexus—and the smaller parachute strapped to her chest would open in the nick of time to save her.

If both chutes failed, she was supposed to steer for open water, turning in midair and angling her drop away from their calculated landing site. It would be wasted effort, Ross decided, even though Johnny assured her there were cases of skydivers landing in water who managed to live.

She reckoned the stories were true, but they would serve chiefly as a distraction during her last hellacious seconds of life, before she struck the earth or the solid surface of the ocean with sufficient force to break every bone in her body.

Ross nearly lost it when she burst out of the cloud bank and beheld the target stretched below her, like a blown-up painting or a photo of an island with the blue sea all around. She knew precisely where they were supposed to land, at the southern tip of Isla de Victoria, but from her viewpoint it seemed ridiculous to think that she could hit the island, much less a specific quadrant or its wooded mass.

She still had nineteen hundred feet to go before she pulled the rip cord and found out if she would live or die. Meanwhile, Ross thought, she might as well enjoy the view.

Camp Nowhere, Isla de Victoria

THE NEW ACCOMMODATIONS weren't the worst Bolan had seen. He had a roof over his head, four walls, and one small window that admitted sunlight during certain hours of the day. He had no access to the window, since his cage—a real one, welded bars and all—was planted in the middle of a ten-by-seven room. It couldn't have come in through the narrow door assembled, but the bolts were tight enough to slice his fingertips when he attempted to unfasten them by hand.

Bolan wasn't shackled in the cage, and there had been no further efforts to interrogate him after he was moved. The creature named Eduardo was around the camp, somewhere. He came in periodically to look at Bolan, fingering some shiny implement of torture, but until he stepped inside the cage, his threat was too remote to be of any real concern.

And if he came inside, he might be in for a surprise.

Bolan had given them no trouble on the flight, because he hadn't known where he was going, wasn't sure if it was worth the final sacrifice or if he ought to bide his time and find out what came next. He still wasn't positive of their location, but from what he'd seen and heard so far, he had narrowed it down to one of two possibilities.

The camp he occupied was either on Isla de Victoria itself, or on some nearby island where Maxwell Reed's rebels had a combat staging area. From the reactions of those around him whenever an airplane passed overhead, he suspected the former. Fear of air strikes went along with doing business in the enemy's backyard.

Why would they transfer him to Isla de Victoria, the middle of an active war zone? There were quicker ways to kill him, and it didn't seem the move had anything to do with stepped-up efforts at interrogation. Quite the opposite, in fact, since he'd been left alone aside from the delivery of starchy meals on metal plates. He plainly had no inside knowledge of the present battlefield, no useful information on Reed's enemies.

Which led him to conclude that he was bait.

For whom? That question posed no challenge. Who else could his captors hope to lure with Bolan dangling on a hook, except the other members of his team?

He hoped the others would be smart enough to stay away, but he feared they would follow him—not only to free Bolan from captivity, but as a natural extension of their mission. If the enemy had shifted his command post to the island, Johnny would pursue him. That was simple logic. And it was enough to ruin Bolan's appetite for greasy stew.

He pushed away the plate of slop and wiped his fingers on the dirt floor of his cage. He'd thought of tipping the cage, but found it was too heavy. Furthermore, it seemed that metal stakes anchored its corners to the earth. Traces of rust told him the locals hadn't built the cage especially for him, and Bolan wondered idly who else might have shared the grim retreat— or who else it was waiting for.

His mind never strayed far from thoughts of escape, but no opportunity had presented itself. If they removed him from the cage, or even opened it to come inside, then he might have a chance. So far, however, Bolan's jailers seemed content to slide his plates through a two-inch gap beneath the door and wait for him to pass them out again in the same way.

What would he do if he could get his hands on one of those who'd caged him—or a weapon? There was no firm plan in Bolan's mind, since he'd been hooded on arrival in the camp and didn't know its layout, access routes, or any other worthwhile information. Still, he didn't need a complicated strategy.

Given a chance, he'd kill as many of them as he could, raise hell with every means at hand until they cut him down. If he could flee the camp and slip into the wild, so much the better, but he wasn't counting on it. Sometimes, it was all a soldier could accomplish just to take some of the opposition with him, as he slipped into that long, last night.

Maybe.

The Executioner was nothing if not patient.

Sitting in his cage, he waited for the enemy to make a fatal slip.

Victoriana, Isla de Victoria

"IT IS BEYOND my understanding," Grover Halsey said, "how this pathetic band of ragtag rebels can elude you so persistently. Will you explain that, please, William?"

General William Drake, resplendent in his best dress uniform with medals gleaming on the tunic, hesitated prior to answering his president. Diplomacy was not his strong point, and he now faced a dilemma of his own creation. Halsey was employing Drake's own words, insults demeaning their mutual enemies, to emphasize Drake's failure as a field commander.

"Mr. President," he said at last, "we've known for some time that Reed's guerrillas are supported, trained and financed by outsiders. These subversive elements despise Your Excellency, and they seek to capture Isla de Victoria for selfish purposes. They're criminals, in fact, not revolutionaries as they would pretend."

The president replied, "Our troops are well-equipped and well-trained, are they not?"

"Yes, sir. They are."

"And so, my question stands. Why can't we find these gangsters—these criminals, as you call them—and destroy them?"

"Sir—"

"It's come to my attention, William, that a recent shipment from the United States has been—what should I say? Misplaced in transit. Can you tell me what's become of it?"

Drake felt the floor begin to tilt beneath him. "At the moment, no, sir. We're investigating, as you would expect, but—"

"I expect no less than total loyalty from my subordinates!" The shout stung Drake as if he had been slapped across the face. "What I do not expect, and will not tolerate, is treason and corruption! Do we understand each other, General?"

"We do, sir. Certainly." Drake's hands were trembling, clenched in fists against his thighs. He'd stiffened to attention when the president began to shout, and now his sense of balance started to desert him, left him wobbling on unsteady legs.

"I hope so, William." Calmer now, thank heavens, but the president was no less grim of countenance. "I don't mind telling you that it would sadden me beyond belief to learn you had betrayed me."

"Sir, I never—"

Halsey raised an open hand to silence him. "I would be saddened, William, not defeated. I believe you know the difference. The penalty for treason during time of war is death, without appeal. You understand?"

"I do, sir. Yes, of course."

"I'm glad. You'll find my missing weapons, then, within the next twelve hours. No excuses, no delays, and no diversions. I presume that's clear enough."

"It is, Your Excellency!" the general replied.

"And I want these ragtag rebels found, William. Found and destroyed. Pathetic as they are, for all their foreign aid, it should be no great challenge for an officer of your proved ability."

"No, sir. I mean, yes, sir!"

"That's gratifying, William. Shall we say twenty-four hours? Twelve for the guns and twelve for the rest?"

Only one answer was acceptable. Drake nearly choked on it. "Yes, sir."

"You please me, William." Halsey's smile lit up the office. "I've no doubt you'll succeed. If any more incentive is required, remember that your life depends on it."

"Yes, sir!" Drake managed a salute without collapsing, clicked his heels and left the office with whatever tattered dignity he still possessed. The door swung shut behind him with a sound of grim finality.

Twelve hours to retrieve the missing arms, twelve more to find the rebels and destroy them. It was ludicrous. Drake had a vague idea who might be responsible for pilfering the weapons—more than that, perhaps, though he could not admit it under penalty of death—but how could he retrieve them after they'd already been sold to members of the other side?

It might not be too late, he told himself. If nothing else, he could apply pressure to certain likely suspects and discover what they had to say. Perhaps the president would accept their confessions and their broken bodies in place of the missing weapons.

Perhaps.

As for the rest of it, the order to defeat their enemies by the next evening, Drake knew it was hopeless. After eighteen months of struggle in the mountains and jungles of Isla de Victoria, who could promise such a miracle?

He could. In fact, he had done so.

But he could not deliver on that promise.

Drake supposed President Halsey had decided to get rid of him, and so had engineered this stratagem to do the job. Drake had three choices now. He could attempt to flee the country, with whatever he could carry in a suitcase, although he reckoned he'd be watched nonstop by Halsey's spies.

The second option: Drake could give up and admit defeat, prepare himself to meet death in the knowledge that he'd done his best for his God, homeland and president. That choice had limited appeal.

The third option was to succeed, fulfill his promise by locating and destroying the rebels who threatened both his nation and his life.

But how?

As Drake followed his escorts to his armored limousine, it suddenly occurred to him that there might be a way. With just a little help from someone in the rebel ranks, perhaps, he might yet find a way to save himself.

IT WAS A ROUGH RIDE, plunging through the forest canopy. While vines and branches whipped around him, birds and monkeys scattered in a riot of confusion, shrieking panic as they fled. The forest tried to snare him, and it finally succeeded, when his chute snagged and he jolted to a halt, some thirty feet above the deck.

He was prepared for that, however, measuring his distance from the nearest tree trunk as he dangled in midair. A sturdy branch was almost within reach, attainable if Johnny could propel himself three feet or so in its direction.

Kicking gently, then with greater energy, he arced through space like a child on a playground swing, reaching out for the branch that might save him and offer a path to the ground. Johnny's fingertips grazed it, then swept out of touch on the back swing, accompanied by the sound of fabric ripping somewhere overhead.

Next time, as he swung toward the branch, he grasped it with both eager hands and threw a leg over its girth, hauling himself aboard. As soon as he was settled, Johnny shed the quick-release parachute harness and let it fall away. He wouldn't have a chance to bury it, as he'd been trained to do, but any searchers would be forced to scan the treetops, instead of looking on the ground below.

And by the time they found his gear suspended thirty feet above their heads, he'd be long gone.

Johnny descended cautiously, watching for snakes and stinging insects as he made his way to the ground. The mossy bark slipped through his fingers here and there, but he clung fast by sheer determination. Finally, when he ran out of branches, he was forced to drop the last twelve feet and landed in a crouch.

"You stop for coffee on the way, or what?" a voice behind him asked.

He turned to find Ross watching him from twenty feet away. "They didn't have my brand," he said. "Did you have any problems, coming down?"

"You mean aside from frostbite and that cool part where my whole life flashed before my eyes? Nothing to speak of, thanks."

"What happened to your gear?" he asked.

"I stashed it in a hollow tree back there," Ross said, nodding vaguely behind her. "Covered it the best I could and cleaned up my tracks so they won't know where I went from there. Yours didn't make it down, I see."

"Fortunes of war. We'd better get a move on in case someone spotted us," Johnny said, consulting his compass. He calculated a course that would follow the island's northwest-southeast axis. "It's that way," he told Ross, pointing through the trees.

The major problem with their plan was the relative lack of battlefield intelligence on Isla de Victoria. Maps showed them where the towns were, none of them quite large enough to qualify as a city on the scale of anything in the U.S. or South America, but more important were the things those maps did not reveal.

Johnny didn't know where the Victorian Liberation Movement's guerrillas were headquartered, or where they had their outposts. He didn't know which villages were used as command posts by government troops on the defensive. Above all else, he didn't have a clue where his brother was being held— or if Mack was anywhere on the island.

Desperation had brought him to this clearing in the forest, and Johnny was bound to continue in spite of the risks. He would not simply launch himself and Ross into the wilderness, however, without some vestige of strategy. To that end, they'd decided—Ross with reservations—that they should proceed from touchdown on a course that would take them, ultimately, to the island's capital. They would stop at the nearest settlement along the way, where Johnny was certain they would find either their enemies or someone who could put them on the proper trail.

"Let's go," he said, and set off through the forest shadows with a determined stride, trusting that Ross would follow him.

She did, and in another moment they were swallowed by the shadows.

7

Barry Joslin wiped his sweaty face with the back of one hand, avoiding his eyes, and wished for the hundredth time that he was somewhere else, doing almost anything but chasing phantoms through the jungle on a steamy summer afternoon.

Still, this was what he knew the best.

This was what paid his bills.

"Start looking anywhere in here," he said to Samuel Folkes, his native counterpart and second in command. Joslin supposed he'd never quite get used to black men with British names on a Caribbean island, but that was the way of the world.

"They could be anywhere ahead of us from this point on," Joslin continued, waving the twin muzzles of his M-16/M-203 vaguely toward the wall of forest ahead. "That's if they even exist."

"Parachutes were seen," Folkes replied stiffly.

"Parachutes were reported," Joslin corrected him. "That ain't the same thing at all."

"Why are we here, then?" Folkes challenged.

"You know the answer to that, same as I do," Joslin said. "It's orders. We check what we're told to."

"But you don't trust a native report. Is that it?"

"I trust myself," Joslin answered. He raised his weapon in both hands and held it close to Folkes's face. "And I trust this, at least until it fails me. Quick! The rest of you fan out and start the sweep. Remember we're looking for parachutes and jumpers. Don't forget to check the trees above you. Stay in sight of one another now and don't get lost. Keep quiet, unless you find something. Move out!"

They formed a ragged skirmish line and started moving through the forest that way, taking their time, no hurry in the suffocating heat. There had been sightings of some parachutes, reported from a village to the west, supposedly descending on this general vicinity, but there'd been no contact, no confirmation. Joslin remembered the incident two months earlier, when one of his patrols claimed their point man was snatched up and carried away by an eagle the size of a crop duster. They'd brought his rifle back to prove it, as if that meant anything. Joslin had marked him down as a deserter, with the usual hundred-dollar bounty on his head.

Big Bird and skydivers for pity's sake.

He would have laughed it off, except the scuttlebutt said some unfriendly visitors might soon be dropping in to pay a call. Something about the stranger Tripp had locked up at the base camp, Joslin guessed, but it was need-to-know and he'd been kept out of the loop. Even if he took it with a grain of salt, that didn't mean he'd slack off on his job.

A careless soldier had no prospect for longevity, especially when he was in the middle of a half-assed civil war.

The sky was clouding over, deepening the forest shadows that surrounded him and making Joslin work that much harder at peering under ferns and twisted roots, looking for evidence that jumpers might have landed here and maybe had been smart enough to bury their equipment. He hoped it wouldn't rain. The rain on Isla de Victoria did nothing to relieve the cloying heat and humidity, though it did a fair job of turning the jungle floor into boot-sucking porridge. It was bad enough already, with the flies, mosquitoes and leeches. When it rained—

"Over here!" someone called from his left, and then repeated it. "Over here!"

Joslin scowled and veered off course, moving toward the source of the cries. When the soldier raised his voice a third time, Joslin snapped back at him, "Can it, for Christ's sake! I heard you the first time!"

He didn't know the soldier's name. A corporal by his stripes, he was standing in the shadow of a giant tree that had been partly hollowed out by lightning, insects, scavengers— who gave a damn? Inside the hollow, formerly concealed by some uprooted ferns the soldier had been smart enough to spot and clear away, a parachute and harness had been tucked away from prying eyes.

"I'll be goddamned. You take the honors, boy," he told the corporal. "The rest of you, gather round now. It's confirmed we have at least one jumper, and there may be more. We don't know who they are or what they want, but we'll assume they're hostile. We're on red alert. The sweep continues. Keep it sharp."

He felt Folkes watching him and wanted to ignore it.

Joslin grimaced as the first fat raindrop struck his scalp.

ONE MOMENT IT WAS sprinkling rain—large, scattered drops that missed more often than they hit, pattering on foliage overhead and on the earth below—then, in the next, the heavens opened and a deluge soaked them to the skin.

"Guess that's why they call it the rain forest," Ross ventured, raising her voice to be heard above the din of water pouring through the canopy.

"The good news," Johnny said, "is that it's wiping out our tracks."

He didn't have to tell her the bad news. Their visibility had been reduced to feet, instead of yards, and even that was spotty with the volume of water drenching their faces, making them constantly blink their eyes clear. At the same time, their progress was retarded by the pummeling rain. It left them feeling battered and bruised, and turned the ground to sucking mud beneath their feet. In places, rushing streams now took the place of game trails and made footing all the more precarious. They slung their weapons muzzle-downward, to prevent the barrels from filling with rain, and Johnny wished that he'd remembered the jungle fighter's trick of packing condoms that could keep the muzzle dry.

Each step he took was costly now, in terms of strength and energy, as well as time. It would be easier to lose his bearings in the downpour, and he checked his compass every dozen steps or so, squinting to read its water-beaded face in the deepening murk. Each fifth or sixth time that he checked it, Johnny had to correct his northwesterly course. The brutal rain and running water underfoot seemed bent on driving them southwest, toward the storm-thrashed Caribbean.

Johnny didn't know if anyone had spotted their descent, or if they were being pursued, but he couldn't shake a grim sense of foreboding as they slogged through the hammering rain, stumbling and sliding in the muck with every other step. It seemed almost as if the elements themselves conspired against him, to prevent him from finding his brother and setting him free. Johnny understood how some might give up, abandon the attempt and say to hell with it. He had no more than intuition and pathetic fifty-fifty odds to tell him that his brother was alive, much less within his reach. The lead to Isla de Victoria had been so obvious a trap that most professionals would have refused to follow it.

But those pros didn't have the fate of their last living loved one hanging in the balance, poised on the edge of a trembling razor. They didn't know what it meant to see most of your family claimed by tragedy, to fight your way back from the edge of madness and then see the nightmare beginning all over again.

Only a handful of people on Earth knew that feeling, and Johnny had no time to waste explaining it to those who didn't share the common bond. He was a member of the great Survivors' Club, with dues paid in full, and he would do anything within his power to help his brother now.

Doggedly, refusing to be broken by a force so cavalier and arbitrary as the weather, he kept going. Trusting Ross to hold her place behind him, listening to make sure she was there, Johnny pressed on in search of Mack and redemption, numbly wondering if either was within his grasp.

THE RAIN HAD Barry Joslin in a seriously shitty mood. He didn't mind the clothing plastered to his skin, his wet socks squelching every time he took a step or warm water streaming down his face as if he were standing in a shower stall. What really pissed him off was working with a bunch of half-assed amateurs and knowing that the rain was wiping out whatever traces of their quarry might exist.

They'd found the first abandoned parachute four miles from camp. The second, hanging in a tree some thirty-odd feet off the ground, had been a few yards to the east of the first. There were just the two of them so far, which more or less confirmed the sightings that had launched this ill-fated patrol in the first place.

Where had the jumpers gone?

That was the question Joslin couldn't answer with anything approaching certainty. He was reasonably sure they hadn't headed south, which would have placed them on a dead collision course with Joslin's team. Beyond that, they could have gone anywhere. He couldn't comb the whole damned island with a fifteen-man patrol, no matter how adept they were at reading forest signs. And with the fucking rain...

Trudging along, shaking the water from his face, Joslin attacked the problem logically. If the jumpers hadn't gone south from their LZ, it meant they didn't know about the base camp where the prisoner was caged. If they were truly looking for him but they didn't have a pointer yet, where would they go?

Why not the nearest town?

It was a gamble, but it made more sense to Joslin than the thought of newbies roaming aimlessly through the forest, hoping they stumbled on signs of their friend. At least, if they reached a settlement, they might be able to ask questions, maybe get a lead on where the rebels pitched their tents.

It wasn't much, but it was all he had.

Joslin knew where the nearest settlement was.

"We're going to Johnstown," he told the squad. "You two, Simon and Trent, take the point."

Joslin didn't know why they called the village Johnstown. Probably some guy named John built the first shack and it was all they could think of. That was the least of his problems right now, soaking wet as he was and pursuing phantoms through the forest, hoping there were only two and that he hadn't missed more evidence along the way.

Joslin figured the other members of his team were lazy at the best of times, and absolutely disinclined to mount a thorough search while they were being drenched as if by hoses mounted in the trees. They'd done a perfunctory sweep on his order and came back empty-handed, but Joslin was worried that they might have missed one or more chutes—maybe buried, or shoved in the crotch of a tree above ground. Who could say?

The hell of it was that he could go looking for two men and stumble on two, even three times that many. In which case, he suspected, they would be in some pretty deep shit.

Joslin didn't have details, but he kept his ears open and knew what had been going on in the States, in Panama and Nassau, in Colombia. His side—the side that signed his paychecks, anyway—had taken a series of consistent beatings in the past couple weeks, and all they had to show for it was one guy sitting in a cage who wouldn't tell them squat.

No one would ever mistake Barry Joslin for a coward, but he wasn't wild about the idea of meeting a top-notch strike force in the jungle, when all he had to back him was Folkes and eleven soldiers who, on a good day, were adequate at best.

"No wonder this damn war is taking so long," he muttered to himself.

The trek to Johnstown took them northwest, and Joslin knew it would take them at least three hours. Four was probably more realistic, and it galled him that the men he sought were more than an hour ahead of his team. In the time it had taken Joslin's soldiers to reach the LZ and find the two chutes, his quarry could have covered half the distance to Johnstown.

Then again, they may have headed somewhere else. In which case his great piece of strategy was nothing but more wasted time.

At least one thing was clear: He couldn't go back to Tripp empty-handed—not after finding those parachutes. The smart thing to do would be to call it in, Joslin thought. They might even get help from base camp.

Still slogging through the mulch and mire, Joslin unclipped the walkie-talkie from his belt and keyed the button to transmit.

"Olympus, this is Zion. Do you read me? Shit! Olympus, come back pronto, if you can."

Ross WONDERED whether it was possible to drown while walking through a forest on dry land, but when she glanced down at her sodden feet, she realized the question had been framed improperly. The forest wasn't strictly dry land anymore. Rain had been falling in such volumes that she seemed to be proceeding through a series of muddy streams, splashing along where solid earth had lain beneath her feet an hour earlier.

She hoped Johnny knew where in hell they were going. The plan, if she could call it that, had been to find a native settlement, make cautious contact and determine which side the inhabitants were backing in the island's civil war. Most likely, she supposed, they'd say whatever pleased the latest visitors with guns, but either way they hoped to find out where the rebels had their nearest camp. If they could make it that far, then they had a shot at finding Matt Cooper.

If the word about his being brought to Isla de Victoria was even true.

Too late to sweat it now, she thought. We're here, it's queer. Get used to it.

She almost laughed aloud at that, feeling the sharp edge of hysteria grating along her raw nerves. It was all too much— the HALO jump, the hike, the rain—but there was nothing she could do about it. There was no way out but straight ahead, following Johnny's footsteps to the end of the line.

She wanted to ask Johnny if he thought they had a tail yet,

but she'd have to shout to make herself heard above the rain, and it didn't seem worth the effort. She was spitting out water already, wondering what kind of filth it had picked up on its passage through the forest canopy, worried that she might be slurping some exotic germ or monkey shit or who-knew-what. Not that she could avoid it, in the circumstances, but she clung ferociously to her inalienable bitching rights.

She saw Johnny pause on the narrow river trail and glance back at her. "Are you okay?" he asked.

"Peachy," she said. "There's nothing like a forced march through a flood to make a girl feel springtime fresh, you know?"

He blinked at her, rainwater streaming down his face, then shook his head and set off plodding once again. The fierce smile stayed on Ross's face for something like a hundred yards, before it was washed away and she resumed her focus on the simple act of following the rain-drenched figure through the trees.

ANOTHER HOUR, Johnny thought. At least.

Despite the storm's disorienting impact, he believed they were still on course for the nearest settlement marked on his map. The approach would be risky, but he'd been working on that in his head while he marched along on autopilot through the pelting rain.

He knew white mercs were fighting with the rebel forces on the island. One way to go with the natives, he thought, was to pose as members of the "liberation" army, claim to be lost and ask directions back to their nearest encampment.

The storm would help that story, but the plan had risks attached to it. The locals might be hostile to the rebels, and they might be armed. In that case, he and Ross could find themselves in a firefight with people they were trying to help—that was, if the locals didn't simply take them down by ambush on the trail.

Then again, suppose the village was loyal to the rebels and knew all the white mercs by sight? In that case, Johnny's overture could have an equally bloody result.

The best worst-case scenario that came to mind was a simple stalemate. In that version, the villagers stared blankly at Johnny and Ross, professing ignorance of any rebel camp and leaving them no better off than before they hiked all day through flogging rain to get the door slammed in their faces.

It was a long shot, any way he sliced it, but it was the only plan that he'd been able to devise in the allotted time.

The Victorian Liberation Movement had been waging war on Grover Halsey's loyalists for the better part of two years. It stood to reason that they'd have more than one operational base in the countryside, to avoid putting all of their eggs in one basket. Even if the locals Johnny found were helpful and directed him to the nearest rebel camp, there was still no guarantee that he'd find his brother there.

But at least he'd find someone to ask for directions.

They might not have Mack at the camp he eventually found, but someone would know where the captive was held, or if he was on the island at all. Johnny would have that information from them, no matter what he had to do, and God help anyone who tried to stop him.

Passing between the boles of two great trees, Johnny caught a fleeting respite from the rain and glanced back at Ross. She was lurching a little, as much from fatigue as the sloppy-wet trail, he supposed. They were both beyond tired, with no rest stop in sight, but stopping wouldn't help in this weather, when it was too damned wet to light a fire.

He waited under cover of the two large trees for Ross to

join him. It was slightly drier there, where branches inter-locked above their heads, a drizzle rather than a steady flood.

"Not quitting on me, are you?" she inquired.

"Catching my breath," he said. "How are you holding up?"

"I'll be there at the finish," she assured him. "Maybe not with bells on, but who needs the racket, anyway?"

"Okay. It shouldn't be much longer. I'm thinking an hour or so."

He saw Ross looking past him then, eyes narrowing. "Or maybe not that long," she said.

Turning in the direction of her stare, he saw three black men, shirtless, clad in rain-soaked khaki pants and ancient sneakers, aiming old bolt-action rifles at his face from fifteen yards away.

GENERAL WILLIAM DRAKE was sipping coffee laced liberally with rum and searching for a way to save his job, perhaps his life, when his lieutenant knocked and stuck his head in through the office doorway.

"General? Sir?"

"You see me, Soames. What is it now?"

"A radio transmission, sir. We just intercepted it."

"What sort of radio transmission, then?" Drake wasn't known as patient at the best of times. This day, his nerves were frayed and he was definitely out of sorts.

"A rebel message, sir." Lieutenant Soames had dared to enter all the way, standing rigidly at attention before Drake's bare desk. "From the field, sir."

"Well? What of it?"

"There appears to be...activity, sir."

"Don't tell me they're storming the bloody capital," Drake muttered. "That's all we need." In fact, the notion didn't worry him as much as it would under normal circumstances. With his own neck on the chopping block, why should he be bloody well concerned about a mob of politicians getting axed?

Soames clearly wasn't sure if Drake expected laughter or a straight reply. He chose to play it straight. "No, sir. It seems they're tracking parachutists, sir."

Drake blinked and put down his mug. "What are you saying, Soames?"

"The rebels, sir. They're in a bother over parachutists at the south end of the island. Tracking them, it seems. As if they think it might be our men dropping in."

"We don't have any parachutists, Soames." Stating the obvious, hoping for time to think it through.

"No, sir. Which makes it all the more curious, sir."

Curious, hell. It was bloody bizarre. Who would be parachuting onto Isla de Victoria and tramping through the forest in rebel territory? No one sane, Drake decided. Unless...

"Where was this?" he demanded. "Do we have coordinates?"

"A rough fix on the broadcast, sir. They'll have moved on by now, but we know where they are headed."

"And where is that?"

"They're bound for Johnstown, sir. Apparently, they think the parachutists may be headed there. We don't know why, sir."

"And I don't care why," Drake answered. "If the rebels are en route to Johnstown, so are we. It would make a nice change to have contact on our terms for once, don't you think?"

"Yes, sir!"

"Too right it would. Do we have any notion how many there are in the rebel team?"

"There can't be many, sir. The man in charge was asking for support."

Drake smiled. "Better yet, if they send reinforcements.

They won't know we've listened until it's too late. How many of the helicopters are functional, Soames?"

"Sir, I'm thinking it's four of the six."

That was better than average. The choppers were U.S. Army surplus UH-60 Black Hawks, each with room aboard for four-teen soldiers fully field-equipped. Four aircraft meant that Drake could put fifty-six soldiers on the ground at Johnstown within two hours while reinforcements traveled overland.

With any luck, it just might be enough.

He needed a victory to impress his masters before Halsey yanked the rug out from under his feet. It wouldn't be *the* vic-tory, of course, but any step in that direction had to be a plus, under the circumstances.

And if the attempt turned out to be a failure—well, at least Drake would be going out with a bang, as the Americans like to say, instead of with a whimper.

"I want the helicopters loaded to capacity and on their way to Johnstown at once. No excuses, no delays. The order is to contact and destroy the enemy at any cost. Understood?"

"Yes, sir!" Soames was plainly excited, struggling to re-press a smile.

"All right, then," Drake replied. "What are you waiting for?"

8

There were more than three shooters, in fact, as Johnny discovered seconds after the point men showed themselves. He and Ross were surrounded, with another rifleman on their left flank and two more on the right. Their placement made for neat, no-risk triangulated fire, and there was no hope of disabling all six before they scored a lethal hit.

"Okay, what now?" Ross asked him.

"Just stay cool."

"Good plan."

English was the official language of Isla de Victoria, so Johnny knew he wouldn't have to sweat out a translation. Speaking carefully, despite the rain that streaked his face and dribbled from his chin, he said, "We're on our way to Johnstown for a friendly visit. Do you know the way?"

One of the riflemen responded with a question of his own. "Why does a friendly visit need so many weapons?"

Johnny knew he couldn't duck the question. It was time to roll the dice and see if he got lucky or crapped out. "We're looking for a friend. He's being held against his will by someone on this island, and we mean to get him back."

"Your friend is not in Johnstown," said the spokesman for the firing squad.

"I know that," Johnny granted, "but we need help finding those who have him."

Now the leader frowned. "We do not mix in white men's business."

"We're not asking anyone to join the fight," Johnny replied, "or even guide us to the spot. A pointer's all we're looking for."

"Pointer?"

"Directions. Some advice. That's all."

"Words are the same as weapons," the rifleman said. "Used carelessly, they maim and kill." He thought about it for another moment, then declared, "You will return with us to Johnstown. It will be decided there."

"Sounds fair. Let's go," Johnny agreed.

"Give up your weapons, first," the man demanded.

Johnny pretended to consider it, as if he had a choice. "All right," he said. "We'll want them back, though, if there's trouble on the trail."

That seemed to take the men by surprise. "The way is clear," he told them. "You'll be safe—unless you've lied."

"No problem, then."

Two of the men slung their rifles and came forward to collect the combat gear. Johnny and Ross gave up their rifles, then shrugged out of their web harnesses and bandoliers. The natives who'd disarmed them grimaced at the extra weight and moved more slowly as they backed away.

"Now follow me," the leader said, and turned his back, moving with long strides toward the north.

When they'd been ten or fifteen minutes on the trail, the rain diminished. Johnny barely noticed it at first, and even when it altogether stopped, water still drained and spattered from the canopy above. At forty minutes in, the sun broke through and turned the rain forest into a giant sauna filled with enervating steam.

Each step became a labor then, and Johnny was relieved he didn't have the extra weight of a pack and weapons on his sagging shoulders. The earth, the foliage and his very clothing steamed. He thought the best thing in the world would be to lie down in the mud and rest, but it was not an option.

They had been walking for about an hour when a whistling cry rang out ahead and brought their escorts to an instant halt. The man in charge of the patrol responded with a yelp that could have been a monkey's or a wounded dog's. On hearing it, a sentry with a double-barreled shotgun cradled in his arms appeared as if from nowhere, huddled briefly with the squad's point man, then vanished once again into the forest murk.

More walking, then, along a trail that seemed to open magically before them. Johnny tried to pick out landmarks, but the trees and undergrowth all looked the same to him. He had his compass, but he reckoned that it wasn't wise to show inordinate concern for their precise location. He could always get a fix when they were in the village, if the locals gave him enough time.

Johnny didn't like being unarmed, but there'd been no way to retain the weapons and survive. At this point, any progress was a bonus. If they had to fight within the next few moments, he would do his best with what he had.

That thought was barely formed when they broke through the trees and came upon a hamlet ringed by forest. Simple houses ranged around a central clearing Johnny took to be the village square—or oval, in this case. The settlement's inhabitants were out in force to greet them, watching as the small procession cleared the wall of greenery.

"Welcome to Johnstown," said the leader of their escorts. "Here your questions may be answered, though perhaps not as you wish."

THE GODDAMNED JUNGLE had it in for Barry Joslin. He was sure of it. First rain that nearly washed him off his feet and left him spluttering, then muggy heat that made him sweat through clothes already soaked and sapped the best part of his energy.

Next time, he thought, I want the fucking desert. Or maybe Antarctica.

They were making fair time, even so. Joslin and Folkes both knew the way to Johnstown, as did every member of their team. It wasn't a question of finding their way through the forest, but rather taking time to do it right, without a lot of clamor or overlooked clues on the way.

"Clues my ass," the mercenary muttered to himself, scowling. The rain had wiped out any trail they might have found, and there'd been no more gear discarded on their route of march. Joslin still didn't know if they were stalking two people or ten, but he kept his fingers crossed and hoped for small numbers.

The power of positive thinking.

Joslin's tracking skills weren't the greatest—he trusted the locals for that—but at least he knew where they were going. Whether it had been the right choice was an open question at the moment, but they had to go somewhere, and Johnstown was the best choice for a start. Granted, it would've made him feel better if there'd been something more concrete to tell him they were on a solid trail—

And then, there was.

The team's scout gave a whistle, something like a parrot

with his balls caught in a nutcracker, Joslin thought, and waved at them to hurry up. When Folkes and Joslin reached him, the scout was pointing at some smears and gouges in the mud.

"After the rain stops, people pass this way," he said.

"You're sure about that?" Joslin challenged him.

"See for yourself."

Joslin bent closer to the ground, wishing he had the Davy Crockett gene required to make sense out of what he saw. Was that a heel print, or a hoof mark from a forest hog? He couldn't have decided if his life depended on it—which it might, if there were soldiers up ahead planning an ambush on the trail.

"How many would you say?" he asked the scout.

The native's shrug was eloquent. "Not many. Eight or ten."

Terrific.

That would make their forces nearly equal if they tangled in the jungle, without reinforcements from Tripp. How in hell had they missed six to eight parachutes? The rain hadn't been *that* bad, for God's sake. There was no way to account for it, unless...

"Still heading for Johnstown, I take it?" Joslin said.

His guess paid off with a nod from the scout. "That's affirmative, sir."

A welcoming committee had been waiting for the jumpers, to escort them.

"Looks like our neighbors have some hanky-panky on their minds," he said.

Folkes frowned at him, missing the reference. "Hanky-panky?"

"Mischief," Joslin clarified. "Or worse, in this case. I'd call it collaborating with the enemy."

"We are proceeding, then?"

"Damn right. The faster the better. Maybe we can overtake them on the way."

That wasn't likely, though, Joslin grudgingly admitted to himself. Natives from Johnstown would know half a dozen shortcuts through the forest that would give them an advantage in a footrace. Joslin didn't fancy tackling the whole damned village with his twelve-man team, but Tripp had told him there were reinforcements on the way. He could have radioed to double-check their ETA, but that might make it seem like he was wimping out.

"Let's go," he snapped. "We're burning daylight."

THE VILLAGE DIDN'T SEEM to have a chief, per se. Ross waited with Johnny in the central clearing, surrounded by faces ranging from hostile to simply curious, while the patrol leader vanished, then returned moments later with a smaller, older man. She guessed that the elder—the mayor? headman?—hadn't come out with the rest to see them right away, because it would have been undignified.

If not for protocol, Ross wouldn't have guessed he was anyone special. The man in charge wore no ceremonial garb or insignia, nothing Hollywood had conditioned her to expect from a leader of "natives." His denim shirt and khaki pants were clean and relatively dry, despite the forest's simmering humidity. He wore a floppy cap, gray tweed that nearly matched his salt-and-pepper hair above a pair of wire-rimmed eyeglasses. He spoke to Johnny.

"I am Arthur Holmwood. Johnstown's people have empowered me to speak for them. What brings you here?"

"Your men," Johnny replied, "but we were headed in this direction when they found us."

"Why?"

"I'm guessing that your man already told you that."

"I would prefer to hear it from your lips," the old man said.

This was the dicey part. If Johnny misjudged the loyalty of these villagers, he and Ross could be finished in a hurry. He had to take the chance. "A friend of ours was kidnapped by the rebels who are making war against your president. They brought him here, to Isla de Victoria."

"Why here?" Holmwood asked.

"They were hoping that we'd follow."

"As you have."

"That's right," Johnny said, "but we're playing their game with a twist. They missed us on arrival, but I'm guessing someone's tipped them off by now. Whether they're tracking us is anybody's guess. We need to find their base camp, and figured someone in a nearby settlement would have a fix on where they've put down roots."

Holmwood was frowning as he said, "You took the risk of leading them to us?"

"Not really. First, if they've been operating in the neighborhood for any length of time, they already know where you are. Second, we were trying to keep it discreet, until your people picked us up."

"You are correct, in part," the village leader said. "We know these men and they know Johnstown. Twice they've come at night and taken people from their homes. It's why we now post guards on the approaches to the village."

"Why were people taken?" Ross inquired.

"The first was a young woman," Holmwood answered. "We have not seen her again. Perhaps she satisfied their appetite. The other served them sometimes as a guide, for pay. It was his choice, but I believe he saw too much of what they do and changed his mind. We found him in the forest, when they finished with him."

"So, you're not exactly friends of theirs," Ross said.

"They come here now at peril of their lives," Holmwood replied.

"Sounds like we're on the same page," Johnny interjected. "If you could point us toward their base camp, we'll be on our way and you can just forget—"

"Too late," the village elder said.

"How's that?"

Holmwood relieved the sudden tension with a smile. "It is too late today for you to go. It will soon be night. The place you seek is fifteen miles away, on paths you could not find in darkness. You should stay here and share a meal with us, then set off in the morning."

"I appreciate the offer," Johnny answered, "but—"

A high-pitched, yelping cry resounded through the forest, coming from the general direction they had followed on their own approach. Holmwood immediately stiffened. "They have found you," he announced. "A war party is on the way to Johnstown as we speak."

Ross felt the hairs bristling on her nape. "We really need our weapons now," she told the village leader.

He considered it, then turned to his left and nodded. The riflemen who'd lugged their gear to Johnstown bustled through the press of bodies, coming to return it. Ross slipped on her combat harness first and buckled it in place. She took the bandoliers, grateful for their weight instead of cursing it. The CAR-15 felt good and solid in her hands, better after she'd checked to see that it was loaded.

"Okay," she said, as Johnny finished buckling his pistol belt. "So, what's the drill this time?"

THE LEADER OF the scouting party who had brought the strangers back to Johnstown now regretted finding them. He wished even that he'd killed them in the forest—anything, in fact, to spare his village from the danger now advancing toward its very doorstep.

He listened as the village elder issued orders to his people. Holmwood never raised his voice. There was no point in shouting, he insisted, if the speaker and his words were not respected in the first place. Now, despite the urgency of what he had to say, Holmwood was still soft-spoken, forcing those around him to be silent if they wished to hear.

"I would not have them in the village if we can avoid it," Holmwood said. "Above all, I would not expose our people to the risk. Whether these visitors have brought the danger to our doorstep, or if we ourselves have summoned it, I cannot say. But it is time for us to act without delay."

Robert Grant felt the heat rise in his face at the implied rebuke. He'd done no more than what was reasonable, bringing the strangers back to Johnstown for Holmwood to judge them, but now it seemed he may have imperiled the village and everyone in it. For that, he would gladly atone, but the elder's next words still surprised him.

"Robert, you will show the strangers where they need to go in search of whom they seek. Take your men with you, and be ready to defend yourselves. I will lead the others to a safer place, until this threat is past. If we are fortunate, perhaps our homes will still be here when we return."

Johnny frowned at those words and said to Holmwood, "You're going to let them march through here and rip off whatever they want?"

"There may be damage if we leave," Holmwood replied. "But if we stay and fight, our homes will surely be destroyed."

"I wasn't saying you should fight them *here*," the white man said. "If it was me—"

"It is not you," Grant interjected angrily. "This place is not your home. You don't belong here. You bring death to us without apology, and you insult the elder of our village, as if you—"

"Enough!" As Holmwood spoke the single word, he stepped between them, facing Grant with an expression that was one part anger, two parts disappointment. "We have no time to waste on bickering."

The white man frowned and held his weapon close. He told Holmwood, "I was about to say that we could meet them on the trail and shake them up a little, maybe keep them out of Johnstown altogether."

"Even if we win the fight," Grant said, "they will return. The bad ones always return and punish the helpless."

"Are you helpless?" the stranger asked. "I see rifles here and men to use them."

"We're not warriors," Holmwood told him. "We survive by staying out of wars, not leaping into them for no good reason."

"I'd say you have a reason, when the enemy comes knocking on your door," the white man said.

"Because of *you!*" Grant flared.

"We weren't here when they took your friends away," the woman said. "I never heard of Johnstown before today, but you've been ducking and dodging these people for nearly two years. Maybe it's time you stood up for yourselves."

"An hour in the village, and you tell us how to live? When we should die? How typically American," Grant said, sneering.

"It is decided," Holmwood said before the strangers could reply. "I take the people north. Robert, I hope you will assist them, but I don't command it. Let your own best judgment be your guide."

It was a slap across the face, and Grant accepted it. "I will remain," he said, then raised his voice. "Men without families who would assist us, fetch your weapons now. Guns only!"

Half a dozen turned and bolted for their quarters. As he watched them go and felt the strangers watching him, Grant wondered whether any of them would survive the next few hours.

WHEN THE LAST of the retreating villagers had vanished into the forest shadows with their pitiful belongings, Johnny turned to face the seven who remained. Their leader wore the same hostile expression they had seen when he stopped them on the trail. The others seemed more open, but he guessed they'd jump whichever way their leader went—and that could be a firefight on the spot if Johnny didn't try to bridge the gap between them.

"You don't want us here," he said, stating the obvious, "and frankly, Johnstown wasn't on my list of places that I couldn't wait to visit. Now, the trouble is we *are* here, and the enemy's aware of it. They're coming here, whether we go or stay. The chances are that if they find Johnstown evacuated, they'll destroy it out of sheer frustration. We may be able to prevent that if we meet them on the trail, but I can't guarantee your safety or the safety of your homes, no matter what we do."

"You'd have us meet them in the forest?" Grant asked.

"That's right," Johnny replied. "Only a fool fights in his house if he can take the battle somewhere else. You know the forest like your own backyard. I'm hoping you know it better than they do."

"They aren't from our village," Grant told him. "Some of them are white men, like you."

"So let's test them and find out what they're made of,"

Johnny urged. "What we need's an ambush site, as soon as possible."

"You'll follow me?" Grant asked him, skeptical.

"We're in your hands," Johnny replied.

Grant frowned at that, then nodded once and said, "This way." He ran from the village, southward, with the other native shooters trailing him, while Johnny and Ross took rear-guard.

Grant stopped a quarter-mile south of the village, where the trail was still clear-cut, but jungle pressed in close on either side. It seemed as good a place as any for an ambush. Several fallen trees provided cover on the flanks, while tangled undergrowth offered concealment.

"Too bad they don't have Kevlar plants out here," Ross quipped, as they were fanning out to vantage points on each side of the trail.

Johnny agreed with her, knowing the ferns and shrubs would offer no protection from a bullet. But their enemies faced the same disadvantage. At least the home team had the slim advantage of surprise—or should, unless their adversaries proved more clever than anticipated.

How many would there be? How were they armed? Had they been wise enough to call for backup? Would they use the trail, or spurn it as too obvious and find another angle of attack?

It troubled Johnny that he had answers to none of those questions. The most he could hope for, aside from survival, was a chance to question one of the hunters to see if he knew where Mack was.

And if he's still alive.

They settled in to wait. Johnny and Ross were positioned at opposite ends of a massive log that lay parallel to the trail on its eastern flank. Johnny could see the trail well enough, for a distance of thirty yards or so, but it wouldn't take much for moving targets to elude him in the forest.

Touch-and-go, he thought. Like always.

After fifteen minutes lying in the weeds and listening to insects hum around him, Johnny heard a different sound. He strained his ears, and in another moment recognized the noise of human beings trying to be silent in the wild. It seldom worked and never perfectly. Despite their best effort, there were always leaves to rustle, twigs to snap, and dirt to scuff. Even with their equipment taped and shrouded, creeping men still occupied space, displaced air and caused movement around them wherever they went.

These particular stalkers weren't bad, but they weren't invisible, either. They still had to breathe, sweat and put one foot down in front of the other.

Johnny watched them moving through the forest, single file along the trail. He made out only one white face, and that was daubed with camouflage cosmetics. It appeared to be a small patrol, making for nearly even odds.

He watched the point man through his rifle sights, waiting for the perfect mark, then gave the trigger of his CAR-15 a loving squeeze.

TRIPP HAD INSISTED on leading the strike team himself, stacking it with mercs he trusted. One of them for every four native soldiers—a total of twenty in all. It was the best he could do while maintaining security at his base camp and still making decent time through the forest.

They could have used choppers, but manpower would have to do it this time. Tripp knew they were bucking the odds, a long run for no reason if they got there too late, but he still had to try. He might not get another chance to snatch up more interrogation subjects, someone he could use as leverage against the tough guy in the cage.

But he would have to find them first. While he double-timed toward Johnstown with the troops around him, running in the middle of the pack for safety's sake, Tripp hoped that Barry Joslin hadn't screwed things up.

He could have waited, damn it, to approach the village, but that was a judgment call. Too late to fault it now. Tripp hadn't ordered him to wait because he feared the enemy would slip away once more and leave him clutching empty air. He couldn't let that happen.

Not again.

So they ran, past the point of exhaustion, and into the zone where movement becomes automatic, where numbness set in. The forest worked against them, with suffocating heat and the ground still slick from the torrential rain. They fell, got up and fell again. Mud-covered, nicked and bleeding by thorns they had no time to duck and avoid, bruised by impact with trees and the ground, they ran on. It was a tribute to their training—and perhaps Tripp's leadership—that each of those who fell got up again.

At last, after what seemed a torturous eternity, they heard gunfire ahead. Tripp called a halt, gasping for breath, and huddled with the men of his exhausted strike team.

"This is it," he told them, speaking through clenched teeth to keep himself from gasping like a stranded fish. "We don't know what we're getting into, but your friends are fighting for their lives. The men they're up against want to prevent your president from taking back his rightful place. It's tempting to destroy them when you have the chance, but we need prisoners, if possible. Protect yourselves, but keep an eye out for potential POWs."

All around the huddle were cautious nods of acquiescence and weary snarls as they prepared to fight.

"All right," Tripp goaded them. "This is the real thing, people. Get your ragged asses into gear and move!"

They jogged off through the evening shadows toward the sounds of firing and the wink of muzzle-flashes. Tripp went after them, not dogging it, but happy to let someone else go first. It was a field commander's duty to preserve himself in order to command.

A moment later, as the noise of combat doubled and redoubled, Tripp knew his men had reached the firing line. He still had no idea who they were facing, but he hoped the parachutists were among them. Otherwise, the long run would have been a waste, and maybe worse than that.

For if the jumpers were not here, they had to be somewhere else. Watching the base camp, maybe, and preparing for a strike now that he'd drawn off half the normal force of guards.

Tripp caught himself before the paranoia ran away with him. He had a fight to win and enemies to kill, perhaps a prisoner or two to dissect later, at his leisure.

But he'd have to catch them first, and that meant getting bloody.

He gripped his rifle tightly and pushed forward through the undergrowth, seeking a target for his pent-up rage.

Ross FIRED a short burst from her CAR-15 and watched the target go down thrashing in a bed of ferns that masked him from her view. She reckoned he was wounded, but she couldn't tell how badly, and that left the man a nagging question mark, potentially dangerous.

She ripped another burst of autofire into the wounded soldier's leafy sanctuary, and the thrashing ceased.

Better, she thought, no longer fully conscious of the battle chill that settled over her when she was called upon to kill. It had become a reflex, almost second nature.

The hell of it was, they were outnumbered now. Ross still wasn't sure where the reinforcements had come from, but they were here now and it made the odds dicey. It was not the worst she had faced since the crusade began, but it only took one shooter, one bullet, to bring down the curtain.

So, watch it, she cautioned herself as she sought her next target. The opposition forces knew enough to keep their heads down, for the most part, taking full advantage of the forest and the creeping shades of night. They wouldn't have the sun much longer, and she wondered what would happen then, how they would manage to outwit their adversaries and survive.

Johnny was firing at the far end of the log that sheltered them. Incoming bullets were chipping divots from the bark.

Ross found another target. He was creeping through the brush on her side of the trail, surprisingly close by the time Ross noticed him. She couldn't tell if he was white or black—the painted faces made it all a blur—but he was on the other side, and that was all that mattered when the stakes were life or death.

The guy was stalking someone to her left, seeking a clear shot. Was it Robert Grant? She didn't know the names of the other locals, but they were all in the same boat together, and it could be sinking any minute now.

Ross saw her chance and took it, squeezing off a burst that turned the stalker's painted face into a crimson mask. He slumped into a silent heap without protest. No thrashing this time, only sudden death.

But there was something…

With the gunfire ringing in her ears, it took a moment for

Ross to identify the new sound and to place it. Away to the west, drawing closer by the moment, it would soon overwhelm the sharp sounds of combat.

Helicopters.

"We've got company," she called to Johnny, judging it worth the risk.

"I hear it, too," he shouted.

It had to be more soldiers, could be nothing else, and regardless of which side was pitching in now, she and Johnny would still be prime targets.

She was about to ask him something else, the question barely formed in her mind, when two gunmen burst from the forest on her left and charged her position, bellowing their rage and firing from the hip.

Ross turned to meet them, wondering if their contorted faces were the last thing she would ever see.

9

There came a time in most battles when the combatants paused, however briefly, to ask themselves what in hell was happening. It was the point where chaos overshadowed strategy and best-laid plans went out the window; when minds jammed like untended weapons; when nothing made sense but the hot urge to kill.

Johnny Gray reached that point when the choppers came in. He'd been expecting hostile reinforcements, had acknowledged their arrival on foot from the south, but the airlift was something else entirely. The first bird he glimpsed through the trees was government issue, with olive drab paint and big numbers in white on the tail. That told him he had trouble on a whole new level, and he wasn't sure exactly what to do about it.

Johnny's brother had a self-imposed rule about firing on cops or others he regarded as "soldiers of the same side." Johnny wasn't sure if that applied to regular troops on Isla de Victoria—and he wasn't bound by Mack's ideals in all particulars, regardless—but it struck him that they'd come to help the government in power, more or less, and it made no sense to engage the very troops that were supposed to be his allies.

Which brought him to the problem: No one in officialdom on Isla de Victoria knew who he was, much less why he was there. The island's president had not been briefed, so he could not call off the dogs or ask them nicely not to bite.

It was a recipe for chaos, and the taste was foul.

He scuttled back along the log to Ross's side and raised his voice to say, "We need to split before the regulars set down."

"Those guys are regulars? Aren't we supposed to be on the same side?"

"Too bad nobody told them that."

"Great planning, that. So what's the drill?"

"We need to disengage ASAP," he told her. "Ideally without losing sight of the hostiles."

"Oh, right. Because what could be simpler than that?"

"It won't be simple," Johnny told her, "but it just might—"

He was interrupted by a storm of bullets peppering the log in front of them and whistling overhead. At least two automatic weapons, maybe more, had locked on their position and were laying down the kind of fire that often covered—what?

He rolled out, gaining distance from the epicenter of the fire storm, and came up firing from a new position as two burly soldiers rushed the makeshift barricade. They were firing on the run, but in the wrong direction now, as Ross and Johnny both evaded the incoming rounds. In the delirium of battle now, the shooters didn't even recognize their last mistake.

Johnny took the nearer of the two, punching a short burst through his chest, noting as he went down that he was not a native of the island. War paint might distort his features, but it couldn't mask his race or hide the sandy bristle on his close-cropped scalp.

One of the mercs, then, and one less to worry about down the road. By the time he reached that point of recognition, Ross had disposed of the other point man and was trading short shots with the gunners who'd covered the rush. Johnny palmed a grenade from his belt, pulled the pin and let fly with an over-hand pitch toward the cluster of trees where the muzzle-flashes were most tightly grouped. It was a gamble, granted, but—

The blast was a yard or so to the right of the point he had fixed in his mind for the pitch, but it was close enough. Shrap-nel and shock waves sent the shooters reeling, silenced two of them at least, and gave Ross time to spot another couple as they staggered through the drifting smoke.

Those two were easy, groping for another place to hide, and so shaken in that moment that they didn't realize their backs were fatally exposed. No soldier overlooked an opportunity like that in war, when friendly lives hung in the balance. The time and place for chivalry had never been in combat, on the firing line.

Johnny shot one of the disoriented soldiers in the back, while Ross took down the other. It was grim work neatly done, but it did not resolve their problem with the regulars, whose helicopters even then were settling to the deck outside Johnstown. It was a short jog south from there, and Johnny's flank would be exposed to them as they came on the field.

Unless he found a way to extricate his team and did it soon.

Before it was too late.

TRIPP RECOGNIZED the whirlybirds for what they were: the kiss of death to any hope he'd had of capturing a POW on the pres-ent raid. He wouldn't have the time to verify a kill, much less take prisoners.

It had been all for nothing yet again.

Another bloody waste of time and men.

A plastic whistle hung around his neck against his sweaty chest. Its nylon thong was brown, the whistle likewise, so there'd be no glint that might betray him at an inconvenient moment. Huddled in the shadow of an already bullet-scarred giant tree, Tripp pulled the whistle from inside his cammo shirt and raised it to his lips.

Three short blasts meant retreat. He'd drilled it into every soldier under his command, so there'd be no mistake at a time like this. Of course, he'd hoped there'd never *be* a time like this, when they were forced to cut and run, leaving their dead and wounded on the field—but what the hell?

The main thing was for Tripp to stay alive.

He'd lost track of the second chances the cartel had granted him, but Tripp knew that he couldn't count on any more. His master plan was on the verge of doubling around to bite him on the ass, and there'd be no forgiveness this time, from the men who paid his more-than-ample salary.

Unless he had something to trade.

Tripp blew the whistle and was up and moving southward by the time the third blast echoed through the trees. Bullets were all around him in the muggy air, like angry wasps, but he stayed low and took advantage of the forest as he fled.

He couldn't really call it a retreat per se.

It felt like running for his life.

Or toward his real last chance.

Behind him, Tripp heard the survivors of his troupe trying to break off contact, covering their asses as they disengaged. The racket from the helicopters—three or four of them, at least—had stopped, meaning the birds were on the ground and had spilled their teams into the forest. Any moment now, the sounds of battle would be amplified, and Tripp would know the final conflict had been joined.

Final for now, at least.

Tripp wasn't banking on the Halsey government to do his wet work for him. He'd be grateful if they killed the interlopers, but it wouldn't necessarily solve his larger problem. The soldiers who'd been stalking him for two weeks now hadn't decided on their own to seek him out. They hadn't drawn straws at a party or elected on a whim to make life hell on Earth for some unlucky stranger.

They were *directed* by someone who didn't take the field, someone who pulled the strings, gave orders and sat back to watch the show.

Someone Tripp needed to identify, to sell that name to the cartel in exchange for his life.

And he had only one source left.

He knew the way back to base camp, back to the hut with its cage and the strong, silent soldier inside. Tripp knew how long the hike should take, if he was careful not to fall and break a leg. He wasn't sure how many of the others would return from the ill-fated mission, but he'd nearly given up on caring.

There were more men at the camp, all of them armed. He had a few mercs left to cow the others, keep them steady on the line or shoot them if they ran. He had Eduardo, standing by to give the prisoner a screaming one-way ride to hell, and he had a satellite link to pass on any information they recovered to the men who held veto power on Tripp's life.

Running through darkness now, pausing at intervals to check his compass with a penlight, Tripp could only hope that it would be enough.

THE REBEL TROOPS WERE falling back, or so it seemed. Ross wondered if they might be looking for another angle of attack, knowing the three short whistle blasts had been some kind of prearranged signal. But then the regulars came charging through the line and banished any hope of regrouping.

"Let's go!" Johnny called to her, already slipping away to the south, while the government troops advanced from the other direction, muzzle-flashes blinking dirty orange and yellow in the night.

He didn't have to ask her twice.

An urge to stay and fight the soldiers startled Ross, as much for its perversity as its futility, but she swiftly suppressed it and ran after Johnny, praying that the new arrivals wouldn't have floodlights or night-vision goggles.

The forest floor was treacherous, still muddy from the day's rainfall. It was slick enough to send a careless runner sprawling, or snap an ankle if she put a wrong foot anywhere along the way. And anywhere meant miles, Ross realized, if they were trying to escape from airborne soldiers who could leap ahead of and intercept them.

Somehow, she caught up to Johnny in the dark and gritted at him, "Where are we going?"

"Same plan as before," he replied, slightly breathless. "Find Matt, get him out, kick some ass."

"I mean, where are we going *now*?"

"Right now—"

The man who stepped in front of them was tall and black and held a rifle. Ross was on the verge of shooting him, when a blink from Johnny's penlight showed the face of Robert Grant.

"That's too damned close," she said.

"They're too damned close," Grant answered with a nod toward the ambush site now overrun by regulars and rebels, locked in mortal combat. Muzzle-flashes lit the darkness, gunfire rattling loud while some combatants grappled hand-to-hand. Others were fanning out, advancing through the forest, seeking targets.

"Are your people coming?" Johnny asked him.

"Two are dead," Grant answered bitterly. "I sent the others home."

"Why did you stay?" Johnny asked.

"We can't talk here. This way!"

Ross exchanged glances with Johnny as Grant turned and moved into the darkness. She recognized his attitude and didn't trust it, but she figured they could take him with the odds at two-on-one, if he tried something slippery. Johnny apparently concurred and followed Grant, albeit cautiously, with Ross lagging a few yards farther back.

Her last glance at the killing ground showed flashlight beams and rebels with their hands raised. She was turning from it when a crash of rifle fire announced that there would be no surrender in this conflict.

The gunfire faded as they followed Grant deeper into the forest, farther from the battle. Ross knew it was bizarre to feel regret about the death of men she would have killed herself, if given half a chance, but it was different when soldiers slaughtered unarmed prisoners.

They seemed to walk forever, but she knew it had been less than thirty minutes when they stopped again in another moonlit clearing. Grant stood waiting for them, rifle cocked across one shoulder.

"Now we talk," he said.

"OKAY, WE'RE LISTENING," the white man said. His female companion stood silent, holding her weapon as if she were ready to fire at the least provocation. Grant thought he might be able to shoot one of them if he was very swift and sure, but the other would kill him where he stood.

At the moment, he didn't much care.

"What happened tonight is my fault as much as yours," Grant said.

The white man frowned. "I'd say the rebels had something to do with it."

"I led them back to Johnstown when I took you there."

"On orders from your village elder, right?"

"It matters not. Two of our men are dead. The village may yet be destroyed, by rebels or the army. All my fault."

The stranger frowned and said, "I can't stop you beating yourself up about it, but if you want to help even the score, just point us toward the rebel base camp and then head back to your village. We'll do what we can to settle the tab."

"It's not enough," Grant said.

The woman's tone was sharp, suspicious, as she said, "Excuse me?"

"I must show you where the rebels hide and help you do this thing," Grant answered.

"Why the sudden change of heart?" the white man asked.

"My brother died tonight. By now, my mother knows, or soon she will. I can't go back until I've done my best to punish those who took his life," Grant replied.

"They may be dead already," the white man said. "You should try to let it go."

Grant stiffened. "You say this to me? After you travel from another country to retrieve a friend? How can my own blood matter any less to me than friendship does to you?"

The filtered moonlight let him see an odd expression on the stranger's face. The man and woman shared a glance, as if a silent question passed between them. Finally, the woman shrugged and said, "Okay by me."

Another moment passed before the white man said, "All right. Where do we go from here?"

"Their base camp lies to the southwest," Grant said. "It is approximately fifteen miles from where we stand. If we start now, perhaps dawn will find us there."

"A midnight stroll," the woman said. "Why not?"

"Suits me," her companion replied. Then, to Grant, "I'm sorry for your loss, but if you try to screw us anywhere along the way, don't think I'll hesitate to take you out."

"My brother's blood cries out for vengeance," Grant replied. "For now, your enemies are also mine. As for tomorrow—well, we'll see."

"In that case," the white man said, "after you."

Grant led the way, using his lifelong knowledge of the forest to pick out trails where none were visible, fording swift streams where an unwary traveler might have foundered waist-deep among eels and leeches. Always, he maintained the course and stayed alert for any signs of enemy activity around them. More than ever in his life before, Grant was conscious of the need for stealth and caution, creeping through the night as if the first false step would also be his last.

It gratified him that his two companions also took care to be quiet, watching where they placed their feet and hands. Once, when a viper hissed and lashed out from the undergrowth, the white man struck back with a knife so quickly that the snake was dead before Grant knew he'd drawn a blade.

Grant wished that he had judged these two more carefully before he stopped them on the trail and took them back to Johnstown under guard. He thought, now, that it was a fluke they hadn't killed him and the other men in his patrol. Or maybe it was singleness of purpose.

They had come to do a job on Isla de Victoria, and Grant had interrupted them. The price of that intrusion was his brother's life, and now he had to repay that debt as best he could. Consoling his mother was out of the question, but at least he could assure her that the murderers had suffered for their crime.

My crime, he thought, and wondered whether he would ever shake the guilt that burdened him.

Perhaps at dawn, if they found targets for their guns.

They had been walking for an hour, more or less, when a droning noise sounded behind them, drawing inexorably closer.

"What's that?" the woman asked.

"I think…." Grant hesitated. Waiting. Listening. At last he knew and scowled at the certainty of his knowledge. "Yes!" he said. "They're coming. Quickly! Hide yourselves!"

THE HELICOPTER MADE one pass. There were no floodlights, and it didn't circle back, which told Ross that the airborne troops weren't using infrared heat seekers, either. More than likely, she decided, they were simply traveling from one point to another, without knowing that three targets lurked below them in the dark.

She waited for the chopper to retreat, then listened for the others, staying where she was until both of the men had stirred from cover. Only then did she emerge and join them on the trail that Grant had found.

"That's not what I'd call much of a pursuit," she said.

"There may be infantry," Johnny replied.

"The way that chopper's traveling, he'll leave them miles behind," Ross observed.

"Another leapfrog, maybe."

There was always that. "Okay," she said. "Do we go on or give it up?"

"I'm going on," Johnny said without taking time to think about it.

"Then let's roll out," she suggested, "before something else goes wrong."

The march resumed in darkness over trails she couldn't really see and would have missed without a native guide to lead the way. They marched without respite, pausing only while this or that threatening sound was assessed, pinpointed and dismissed. From time to time, Ross heard some forest dweller keeping pace with them, but not for long. The smell of human sweat and gun oil was enough to put off most creatures and warn them not to meddle with these hunters in the midnight hour.

On and on they traveled, sometimes stumbling on hidden tree roots, at other times feeling their way when clouds and the canopy masked them from moonlight. The helicopter didn't return, and Ross made out no sounds of pursuit from the rear.

All clear, she thought. And instantly the small voice in her head replied, as if.

They were light-years away from safe and sound, she realized. The whole damned island was a death trap.

She trusted Grant—as far as she could see him, anyway—and thought he would deliver them intact onto the doorstep of their enemies. What happened after that was anybody's guess. There'd been a plan, at one time, with a range of permutations, based on whether Matt Cooper was found at the first base they located. Thumbs-up meant a rescue attempt; thumbs-down meant they'd have to snag another source and grill him for directions to the prize.

That plan had taken a hit when they were captured and transported to Johnstown, then fought their way clear and wound up with a guide hell-bent on revenge. Ross didn't know what to expect from that point forward, except for more marching toward mayhem and death. Beyond that, it was anyone's game, and she wasn't even sure she knew the rules.

But she could damn sure make them up as she went.

It was a talent she'd discovered in the past two weeks that might just serve her well for the rest of her life.

However short that proved to be.

Grim-faced and ready for the next collision with the enemy, Ross followed Johnny through the darkness toward their unknown fate.

SOME NIGHTS WERE FLEETING, over in a heartbeat it seemed. A night spent in good company, or in a lover's arms, may seem to last mere moments. Daylight came too soon and banished the waking dream.

Some nights went on forever. Hours filled with longing, pain, anxiety seemed endless. Dawn receded before the watcher's bleary eyes as if the sun had made a promise not to shatter waking nightmares with a ray of cleansing light.

This night felt long to Johnny Gray, and it was getting longer with each weary stride he took along the narrow forest trail. Fatigue now bordered on exhaustion, but he couldn't stop. Their guide might travel on without them if they paused too long, and Johnny's eagerness to see the mission finished had not changed, despite the burden that pursuit was placing on his flesh.

Long nights. Long wars.

Sometimes it felt as if he had been marching through the darkness ever since he learned to walk.

From time to time, he glanced back to be sure that Keely Ross was still behind him. She was stubborn, that one, and no slouch at keeping up. He marveled that Homeland Security would let her go so easily, but that was a bureaucracy in spades: all paperwork and no initiative. He didn't doubt that Ross's former supervisors would do everything within their power to claim credit for the "victory" if she and Johnny pulled it off and managed to survive against all odds.

They'd try.

But if he still had strength enough to lift a hand, they'd fail.

The forest both sheltered them and threatened them, but he knew that it wasn't their foe. The forest was neutral and no less dangerous for that. It didn't care if people came or went, lived or died. The scars they left in passing would eventually heal and pass away. The humans who survived a while would still die in the end, and they would feed the forest in their passing. Their flesh and blood meant no more to the timeless trees than fertilizer carelessly applied.

We've made it this far, Johnny thought. Why not another night, another day?

He wished that he could reach across the miles and learn if Mack was still alive, if he was suffering, or if he still felt any hope. They'd never shared that kind of bond, although he thought of them as close. They'd shared more trauma and togetherness than most blood brothers ever knew in life, but he had never felt a psychic link to Mack, never experienced a premonition that his brother was in danger or in pain without some evidence to prove the case.

Like now.

He knew Mack was in hostile hands, but Johnny couldn't prove his brother had survived the passage from Colombia to Isla de Victoria. There was a chance, however slim, that he and Ross were on a wild-goose chase that would eventually land them both in shallow graves.

But not alone.

The enemy had paid a fearful price already, and they weren't done paying yet. The bloody tab was getting longer by the day, and if he couldn't settle it in full, at least Johnny meant to pay his share.

With interest.

Some pacifists were fond of saying that violence never solved anything, but Johnny knew that was a lie. Throughout the course of history, violence had toppled kings and governments, eliminated tyrants and reformers, settled boundary disputes and questions of religious faith. Some who espoused nonviolence still depended on the raw brutality of others to support their cause.

Bloodshed changed everything. The only question remaining was whether the change was for better or worse. And that answer would not be revealed until all of the bleeding and dying was finally done.

Maybe tomorrow, Johnny thought.

And with a weary heart, he marched on toward sunrise.

10

Something had changed.

Bolan could hear it in the voices passing by his hut, although the voices weren't clearly audible. He picked up words and phrases here and there, but it was more the tone of urgency that warned him of a sudden shift in mood throughout the camp.

He listened, noting how the passersby were mostly running now, instead of walking at a normal pace. They all had things to do, places to be, which was at odds with the normal routine he'd noted since arriving on the island. The troops were upset about something, disordered and nervous. The occasional shouted order was terse, even angry.

Eavesdropping gave Bolan a few clues to work with. He heard the word "dead" several times, and once a short phrase: "They're all dead." Twice he heard mention of "regulars," and once the word "ambush." The name of Garrett Tripp was uttered more than once by the men who served and feared him.

Bolan tried to figure out the puzzle. As a child, he'd read some Arthur Conan Doyle, and he remembered the advice of Sherlock Holmes that it was a grave mistake to theorize before all facts were known. Still, he had nothing else to do, caged as he was, but move the sundry pieces here and there to find out how they fit.

On balance, it was clear there'd been some kind of firefight involving guerrillas and regular troops. He wasn't sure who'd ambushed whom, or who was dead, but Bolan guessed the mood in camp would be jubilant had there been anything to celebrate. It was a safe bet, then, that his captors had tangled with government troops and had gotten the worst of it.

They're all dead.

Did that include Tripp? Had he gone into the field himself to face the enemy? What did it have to do with Johnny, Keely and Jack being hunted on the island by Tripp's men?

The muttered words took on another meaning for him.

They're all dead.

Could that mean Johnny and the others? Bolan didn't think so. Once again, if Tripp's guerrillas had succeeded in their mission, he expected celebration in the ranks, not worried tones and calls to battle stations.

Maybe, though...

One grim scenario tied up the loose ends rather neatly, but he didn't like the end result. In that version, the rebels ambushed Johnny's party, slaughtered them, then stumbled into a government patrol on the way back to camp. Tripp may have led the expedition, or he might be fuming in his quarters over the result.

The Executioner felt no grief yet, since the mental image in his head was simply that. Bolan didn't *know* what had happened; he was guessing and might be far off the mark. Still, if his guess was accurate, he had a duty to the dead and to himself to be prepared.

To even the score.

If Johnny and the rest were dead, it meant that he was truly on his own. There'd be no rescue from captivity, not in time to do him any good. Hal Brognola might plan something from Washington, but by the time he mobilized another team and they tracked Bolan to Isla de Victoria—if such a thing could even be accomplished—it would be too late.

You're alone, he thought. Again.

And he had nothing left to lose.

That thought was liberating and a little frightening. Bolan knew that any move he made against his captors would be fraught with peril, but the same was true of sitting still and waiting for them to decide his fate. There could be only one outcome in that case. If Bolan seized the initiative, at least he'd have a fighting chance.

But not inside a cage.

Unless he found a way outside, the game was over before it began. Tripp's men could shoot him through the bars or simply leave him there to starve. There were no options in the cage. The lock defeated him.

Unless...

A sharp, familiar voice reached Bolan's ears, and in that instant he knew Garrett Tripp was still alive. Alive and angry, snarling at someone who replied in softer tones. The two of them were getting closer by the moment, moving toward his cage.

Bolan was ready when Tripp barged into the hut with the sadist Eduardo behind him. Tripp was disheveled, dressed in wet, mud-stained fatigues. Two worried-looking soldiers crowded the open doorway behind the new arrivals, waiting for orders but keeping their distance.

"All right," Tripp said. "Time's up. One way or another, we're having a chat."

BOLAN ROSE and asked, "What did you want to talk about?"

Tripp barked a bitter, grating laugh. "That's cute. You ought to be a stand-up comic, mister. But you won't be standing up much longer."

"I'll repeat the question," Bolan said.

"Right. You know, I lost a couple dozen men tonight because of you."

"That's fuzzy thinking. I was here the whole time. Ask your watchdogs."

Tripp was nowhere close to laughing now. "You want to play the tough guy, fine. You'll get your chance. Eduardo loves the silent types who think they're strong. Before he goes to work, though, you should know about your friends."

Stone-faced, Bolan asked, "What friends are those?"

"Go on, play dumb. That's fine with me. Just makes it sweeter when you crack." Tripp had to consciously relax his jaw muscles to stop his teeth from aching. "Your friends are dead. My people finished them before the regulars showed up. We didn't get to play with them, the way I would've liked, but what the hell. Dead's dead."

The bastard didn't flinch. Tripp had to give him credit. Self-control up the wazoo, so far.

"Sorry to disappoint you," Bolan said, "but I can't grieve for folks I never met."

"Maybe you'll meet them on the other side," Tripp said. "A day or two from now."

"Looks like you had a long run through the jungle. It can get scary, playing soldier in the dark."

Tripp felt the angry color flood his face. He knew what he had to look like, after stumbling through the forest half the night. His camouflage fatigues were wet and muddy, his boots clotted with muck and debris. Tripp hadn't stopped to wash his face and hands, intent as he had been on talking to the prisoner. Hearing him scream.

"At least I'm here," Tripp said. "That's more than you can say about your friends."

"The friends again. I told you—"

"You don't know them, right," Tripp interrupted him. "Why don't you save the bullshit? Before Eduardo's done with you, I'll know your mother's bra size and the name of every kid who kicked your ass in the first grade."

Bolan smiled at that. "Well, if we're going back that far," he said, "we'd better let your boy get started."

Tripp hesitated for a moment, troubled by the captive's seeming eagerness. He glanced around the cage again, saw nothing out of place. There wasn't much to start with, just a sleeping pallet and the honey bucket sitting in the corner farthest from the prisoner. Certainly nothing the hostage could use as a weapon.

And still, Tripp stalled. Standing with one hand in his pocket, clutching the key to the cage, he made one last attempt. "There's still time to do it the easy way. One chance left, and it expires almost immediately. Why go through the hell of it if you can find a shortcut?"

Bolan met Tripp's stare and held it. "I make allowances," he said, "because I figure you're used to dealing with morons. Still, there's a limit, you know? It's not like you've had anything in mind for me but death, since I checked in. If that's the game, I may as well try it the hard way."

Tripp felt a kind of grudging admiration for the prisoner's defiance, but he didn't let it show. Instead, he let his anger do the talking for him, thinking of the soldiers he had lost that night, the repercussions it was bound to have with his employers.

No more second chances, Mr. Tripp.

"You called it, slick. The hard way it is."

Tripp drew the key ring from his pocket, recognized the cell's key by sight and slipped it into the lock.

BOLAN STOOD HIS GROUND as Tripp unlocked the door to his cell. He shot a sidelong glance at the soldiers in waiting, but they had made no attempt to enter the shed. Eduardo watched him from outside the bars as Tripp swung the door open and stepped across the threshold.

"Tough guy," the mercenary said. "We'll see how tough you really are."

Bolan waited. Eduardo had shifted closer to the cell's open door, dead-dark eyes flitting back and forth between Bolan and Tripp. The tip of his tongue flicked dry lips.

"You're a decent size, I'll give you that," Tripp said, advancing cautiously. "But big and tough are very different things. I think you scared the Russians just by showing up. They can't get used to anybody fighting back. It's how they think, you know?"

Tripp raised his left hand and tapped his temple with the index finger, smiling. Bolan took advantage of the lapse and made his move.

He didn't telegraph the play. Tripp had no warning, not even a blink to let him brace himself. One moment, Bolan stood relaxed; the next, he sprang forward off his left leg, while the right came up to slam Tripp's chest with a flat-footed kick. The impact hurled Tripp backward against the bars with stunning force, and Bolan waded in to nail him with a one-two in the gut.

Eduardo was moving as Tripp doubled over and slumped to his knees. He could have slammed the door from outside, maybe locked it that way for all Bolan knew, but instead he came into the cage. Halfway there, he was drawing a pistol from under his loose, baggy shirt. It was some kind of semiautomatic, stainless steel. Maybe not double-action, because he was thumbing back the hammer, trying to raise the gun and fire.

Bolan was faster, rushing forward with a silent snarl. He ducked below the rising handgun, brushing it aside, and drove his shoulder into Eduardo's solar plexus. Bolan's momentum carried them against the bars, where Eduardo's skull made a dull ringing sound on impact. He almost went limp, but an ingrained survival instinct kept the Colombian from folding. Instead, he hammered Bolan's back with the butt of his pistol, trying to line up a shot from close range.

Bolan countered that move with a head butt to Eduardo's chin, ringing the chimes a second time. His left hand found Eduardo's flailing wrist and pinned the gun above his head, aimed at the ceiling, while his clawed right hand found the enemy's groin. He squeezed and twisted, silencing a gasp of pain with another head-butt to Eduardo's face.

The soldiers were coming. Bolan heard them charge into the shed, one of them cursing, and he knew their first instinct would be to kill. He couldn't trust their self-restraint or any orders they'd received to keep the prisoner alive and fit to talk. They'd use whatever weapons they were carrying, instinctively, and that would be the end of him.

He pulled Eduardo's limp form from the wall of steel, spun him, and ringed the sadist's neck with his left arm. Bolan's right hand disarmed his hostage and palmed the weapon, which he now recognized as a Browning Model 35 Hi-Power, equipped with a 13-round mag. Thumb-cocking it meant Eduardo kept one in the chamber, but Bolan couldn't tell if he'd topped off the magazine to make it fourteen rounds.

The two soldiers hesitated as Bolan turned to face them, holding Eduardo in front. Both had pistols in their hands—a break for Bolan, since assault rifles would have rendered his human shield useless—but they hesitated for an instant, giving Bolan time to pick his target with the Browning.

A silent break was out of the question. If he didn't stop the soldiers here and now, they'd either cut him down in a blizzard of gunfire or bolt from the shed to alert their comrades. Either way, Bolan needed a quick fix to the problem, and his borrowed weapon wasn't sporting a suppressor.

He chose the nearer of the two, a clean shot through the soldier's open mouth that chipped his front teeth going in and exited from the base of his skull. Bolan knew it wouldn't be long before someone turned up to investigate.

The second shooter took a chance. His first round missed, clanged off the bars somewhere behind his target, while the second scored a solid hit. Eduardo flinched and made a gurgling sound inside his chest, then slumped in Bolan's grip.

The Executioner fired again, a double-tap that pitched the soldier over backward, sprawling in the blood his friend had spilled. Almost before he hit the ground, Bolan had finished with Eduardo, tightening his grip and twisting sharply, instantly hearing the snap of parting vertebrae.

He dropped the corpse and hurried back to Tripp. The merc was stirring, wobbling on hands and knees, when Bolan clutched a handful of his hair and hauled the man to his feet. The Browning's muzzle burrowed underneath Tripp's chin.

"You have a choice to make, mister," he told the mercenary. "Do you want to come with me, or shall I leave you here?"

THE SOUND OF SHOTS distracted Captain Bertram Thomas from the task of reinforcing the camp's perimeter. Tripp had demanded it upon returning from the forest, muddy and beside himself with rage or fear, perhaps a bit of both. He wanted more security in case some of the regulars had followed him, and Thomas didn't argue, even though he viewed the threat as minimal. It didn't pay to contradict the white man hired by Maxwell Reed to supervise his nation's war for independence.

Not if Thomas valued his position and his life.

He'd reckoned Tripp and the Colombian were off to grill the prisoner. Thomas had been anticipating screams, but gunfire took him by surprise, particularly when he recognized the sound of two guns firing almost simultaneously.

Some of the soldiers in camp were already drifting toward the prefab hut, moving cautiously with weapons in hand, but they did not rush to the scene of the shooting. Thomas understood their caution, based on personal experience with Tripp and the aura of evil that surrounded his guest, the man called simply Eduardo. Such men had no place in a legitimate military operation, but Thomas had no authority over Tripp or his invited visitors.

The captain moved swiftly, calling orders to the men around him, organizing a dozen of them into an ad hoc rifle platoon. It was his duty to investigate unusual occurrences in camp, and Tripp could not legitimately censure Thomas for doing his job, even when Tripp's own behavior triggered alarms.

Besides, Thomas thought, it might do the mercenary good to find himself facing the business end of a dozen rifles for once. Perhaps he would recall, if only for a moment, that the revolution had some purpose other than his own glorification and enrichment.

And if there was an "accident"…what then?

The thought was fleeting, but nonetheless attractive. Still, Thomas suppressed it as he marched his soldiers through the heart of camp and stationed them outside the prefab building's only exit. There was no more gunfire, nothing at all to be heard from the hut. In fact, the eerie silence disturbed Thomas more than the gunfire.

He had to find out what was happening inside the hut, which might involve some risk. As the southern rebel unit's second in command, Thomas was not allowed to jeopardize himself unduly. Therefore, with a measure of relief he managed to conceal, he chose a private from the ranks and sent him for a look behind the hut's closed door.

Before his soldier covered half the distance, Thomas saw the door slowly swing open, propelled from within. An instant later, Garrett Tripp emerged, still dirty and disheveled, but with bright red blood smeared copiously on his lower face. Thomas was on the verge of calling out to him, asking if Tripp required assistance, when another form emerged.

It was the prisoner, somehow released and armed. The pistol in his hand was pressed against Tripp's head.

Again, the urge came back to Thomas. He could issue a command to fire, dispose of both men in a second, and Tripp's death would be a mishap—friendly fire inflicted while frustrating an escape. It would be clean and easy.

But the moment passed, and Thomas gave no order to his men. Instead, he waited for the prisoner to speak, voice his demands. The captain's next surprise arrived when Tripp spoke up instead.

"Lay down your weapons," he commanded. "Do it now!"

IT WASN'T REALLY GAMBLING, per se, when a player had nothing to lose. Bolan had weighed the odds, deciding that he faced no greater risk outside the prison hut than lingering inside it. Either way, if his enemies came knocking and disliked the answers they received, he'd be little more than a target in a shooting gallery.

Except that this target shot back.

He had three pistols now, the two spares tucked into his

waistband, and a shiny switchblade knife he'd lifted from Eduardo's corpse. The Colombian didn't need it, but a keen cutting edge might serve Bolan well in the forest.

Assuming he made it that far in one piece.

He had given Tripp a choice before they left the hut: cooperate or die. The mercenary understood those terms, and he had the authority—at least in theory—to command the rebel troops. Whether they listened to him or not was another question, and there was only one way to find out the answer.

The hut was more or less surrounded as they emerged. Bolan kept Tripp in front of him, the Browning cocked and pressed against the skull behind the merc's right ear. Three pounds of pressure was enough to do the job, and Bolan had the better part of two pounds on the trigger now.

The camp was mostly dark, no floodlights blazing to betray their presence in the night. Moonlight and the odd lightbulb were ample to illuminate the ring of weapons thrown around the prison hut. Bolan wasted no time counting heads or guns. There were enough to kill him if they tried, and Bolan guessed he could drop two or three before the others put him down.

Long odds, but he still had a hole card left to play.

"Lay down your weapons," Tripp commanded. "Do it now!"

The rebels stood their ground, unmoving. Bolan half expected one of them to fire, a nervous twitch would do it, and unleash a storm of bullets that would send him tumbling after Garrett Tripp into oblivion. He waited for it, tightening his death grip on the Browning's trigger until barely half a pound remained between the bullet and Tripp's brain.

"One twitch," he warned the hostage, "and you're history."

When Tripp spoke again, his voice had gained a cutting edge. "I said lay down those weapons now! That's a direct order!"

Still nothing for another beat, until one of the soldiers on the line signaled for the guerrillas to obey. Slowly, as if they feared they would be shot as soon as they disarmed, the men stooped to deposit rifles on the ground. Bolan assumed that there were more he couldn't see, behind the hut and off to either side, but those in sight soon stood before him empty-handed.

"Captain Thomas!" Tripp called to someone in the dark. "Collect the weapons and remove them to your quarters, on the double!"

At another silent signal from the officer who had to be Captain Thomas, two guerrillas broke formation and began retrieving the rifles, working out in both directions from the center of the line. They passed from Bolan's view on either side, confirming his presumption that he was surrounded, and returned long moments later, each with weapons cradled in his arms and slung across both shoulders. Shoving through the line, the pair retreated toward a hut halfway across the camp.

Bolan had no idea how many guns they'd left behind, clutched in the hands of riflemen he couldn't see, but there was no time to inspect the camp at large. The longer he delayed his exit, Bolan realized, the greater his chance of being cut down by a sniper lurking in the dark.

"We're leaving now," he said to Tripp. "Nobody follows us."

"Which way?" Tripp asked him.

"North," Bolan answered, for no good reason. He didn't know where the camp was located, how many miles separated it from the nearest settlement, or whether the natives would kill him on sight. They might not make it to the camp's perimeter, but Bolan had to try.

Because the only other option on his plate was certain death.

"You heard the man," Tripp told his men. "Stand back and

let us pass. No one comes after us. I say again, no one comes after us!"

They moved out slowly, Tripp's soldiers parting to let them pass as Bolan steered their boss toward the camp's northern perimeter. This was the time to take him, if they were serious about it, willing to sacrifice Tripp and a few of their own. Even bare-handed, they could still drag him down and kill Bolan before he could empty the gun in his hand.

But no one moved.

Instead, they stood rock-still and watched the two men pass from sight, beyond the limits of the camp and into the forest beyond.

"SO FAR, SO GOOD," Tripp said.

"Shut up and watch your step," Bolan ordered, punctuating the command with a prod from his pistol.

The camp was lost to sight behind them now, nothing but forest all around. Its bird and insect sounds told Tripp that dawn was fast approaching. Yet another steaming day would soon begin, and Tripp could only wonder if he'd live to see the sun go down when it was over.

Tripp listened for sounds of pursuit as he moved through the forest, straining his ears to catch footsteps or voices, all in vain. He wondered if Thomas would send a party to find him, or whether he'd take Tripp's last order to heart and do nothing.

Tripp had tried to wink at Thomas as he spoke his final words in camp, but it was dark and he couldn't tell if the captain had seen it. Then again, suppose he had seen but simply chose to ignore it. They'd never been the best of friends. Thomas resented white mercenaries meddling in his country, much less calling the shots in the civil war. Tripp, for his part, had displayed an arrogance not calculated to ingratiate himself with locals. He acknowledged it—a strength or weakness, depending on the circumstances and the point of view—but there was nothing he could do about it if Thomas chose to let him die.

There was an outside chance the prisoner-turned-captor might decide to spare his life, but Tripp wasn't betting the farm on that outcome. When the chips were down, he placed wholehearted trust in no one but himself. The man walking behind him was an enemy, albeit one deserving of respect. They shared no common ground, and Tripp had no reason to think that any plea for mercy would be granted.

What was it that the Bible said?

The Lord helped those who helped themselves, or words to that effect. Napoleon had once suggested that God favored the side with more artillery, but that view didn't suit Tripp's needs at the moment, since he was unarmed, while his captor was packing three pistols.

Still, there might be something he could do to help himself. The timing had to be exactly right, and there would be hellacious danger in it, but he had to try something.

Tripp saw his opportunity ten minutes later. The sky above the forest canopy was lightening from navy blue to charcoal gray, but darkness still prevailed amid the trees and undergrowth below. Their trail was sloping downward at the moment, falling toward a stream they'd have to cross if they continued on their northern course. Tripp had already cleared it twice that night, coming and going from the battle where he'd lost so many men. He knew the water wasn't deep, but it was swift, a downhill rush toward who knew where.

If he could pull it off without stopping a bullet in the process, it might free him from captivity.

Or it might get him killed.

Tripp chose his moment, looking for a patch of muddy trail to make it seem more realistic. Seconds later, when he "slipped," arms flailing helplessly, Tripp blurted out a string of curses, letting gravity take over, tumbling down the slope head-over-heels.

He heard the gunman shout behind him and waited for the bullet, but it never came. Maybe a gunshot seemed too risky in the circumstances, telling Thomas and the rest in camp that Tripp was dead and they could come hunting for the fugitive with no holds barred. Or maybe Tripp was slick enough that his companion on the trail really believed he'd fallen accidentally.

Tripp went somersaulting down the hillside, pushing off with his feet when it seemed he was losing momentum. Vines and bushes whipped at him, tearing his clothing and flesh, but they hardly slowed him. A crashing in the undergrowth above and behind him signaled pursuit, but his lead was substantial and gravity was his best friend.

Tripp hit the water like a cannonball, all foam, and felt the bottom scrape his elbows as he sank. He feared the current wasn't strong enough to carry him, but then it got a grip and he was speeding once again, not tumbling now, but stretched out on his back and going with the flow, blessing the water's chill before it settled deep into his bones.

Screw hypothermia, Tripp thought. I'll take it over bullets, anyday.

The stream took over, sweeping Tripp away from danger and off into the void of the fading night.

BOLAN HAD A CLEAR SHOT from the bank, but caution stayed his hand. Tripp's fall was damned suspicious for an accident, but either way, the man was gone. A killing shot would not have brought him back, but it might tell the rebels back in camp that Bolan was fair game.

What next?

He would keep moving, putting more distance between himself and those who'd caged him, looking for an opportunity to turn the game around on them. He'd done nothing but rest since landing in the cage, so fatigue was not an issue. Every moment that pursuit was stalled, it lengthened Bolan's lead. He meant to take advantage of that head start while he could.

Bolan waded the stream, fighting the current, nearly slipping twice before he reached the other bank and climbed ashore. He didn't linger in the open, rather pushing on into the cover of the trees beyond. A few yards in, he paused once more and listened for pursuers, but heard nothing.

As he walked, Bolan allowed a portion of his mind to dwell on Johnny, Keely Ross and Jack Grimaldi. Whether they were truly dead, he couldn't say. It was a possibility, of course, but Tripp could just as easily have fabricated the report to break him down and make him talk. In either case, Bolan was on his own for now, one man against imposing odds.

He would take in stride whatever happened next. He was armed, though already regretting his lapse in not snagging a rifle when he had the chance. Human contact was his first priority, though cautiously. He couldn't blunder into the first settlement he found, assuming that the natives would be sympathetic to his plight. They could be rebel sympathizers or bandits for all he knew.

And if he didn't find a settlement, what then?

Bolan would make his way back to the rebel camp, in that case, and inflict what damage he could with the tools at hand. It might be a suicide mission, but he would play the cards he was dealt without complaint.

An hour later, well into the forest with a rosy sky above, he picked up sounds in front of him that made him pause, then go to ground. He recognized the telltale noise of people moving through the forest. They were being quiet, but their passage was still audible.

How many?

He couldn't be sure, but with ten rounds in the Browning and two more loaded pistols in his belt, at least he had a fighting chance.

Bolan waited, watching, as a black man with a rifle came into view. There were others behind him, dressed in camouflage fatigues, but Bolan had seen enough.

"Stop there!" he ordered, moving out to block the trail with guns in hand.

"You want to point those somewhere else?" his smiling brother asked.

11

Captain Bertram Thomas was worried. It didn't happen often, which made the event more traumatic. He suppressed the growing sense of dread as best he could, compensated for it by snapping at his men when they stepped out of line—or even when they didn't—but there was no denying the fact that his normal self-confidence was rapidly fading.

It had been three hours and counting since their captive fled the camp with Garrett Tripp, and Thomas felt as if he were paralyzed. Tripp had ordered him not to dispatch any hunters, and while Thomas thought the white man may have winked as he said it, the fleeting tic might as easily resulted from the beating he'd suffered or the pistol grinding into the base of his skull.

So there'd been no search, no pursuit. Thomas had devoted himself to reinforcing the camp with the men and gear he had left, numbingly aware that no one remained to receive his report of the deaths and Tripp's kidnapping. No one was left to advise or assist him.

He was alone, in command of a force already depleted and disheartened by recent events. Some thirty men remained in camp, and they were not the best he'd seen. If the regulars found them today...

Thomas dismissed that thought as defeatist and counter-productive. He would deal with the problems as they came, each in turn, and give his best while he lived. It was a soldier's way to deal with issues individually, tackling obstacles one at a time. The good news was he still had thirty men, all armed, and he would lead them to the best of his—

A shout went up from the camp's northeast perimeter, drawing Thomas from the shadow of his quarters, weapon in hand. He moved toward the point where three sentries stood poised, rifles shouldered and aimed at the tree line. Thomas saw nothing in the shadows, and he wondered if his men were suffering from a hysterical reaction to Tripp's abduction and the recent death of their friends.

"What is it?" he demanded of them. "Who gave the alarm?"

A nervous private blinked at him, reluctant to take his eyes from his gunsights. "I did, sir. There was someone in the trees."

"Some*one*, or some*thing*?" Thomas challenged. "We live in a forest, you know. There are animals and—"

"Hold your fire!" called a voice from the thick under-growth. "Stand down, for Christ's sake, and don't shoot me!"

That voice! Could it be?

"Stand ready," he ordered the sentries. "Do not fire with-out my order. Understood?"

The soldiers muttered variations of "Yes, sir," plainly un-happy that they wouldn't be allowed to spray the jungle with precautionary fire. Thomas recognized the urge, standing with his own rifle aimed at the tree line, safety off, finger tense on the trigger.

"Come forward and be recognized!" he told the disembodied voice.

"I'm coming. Give me time. My goddamned ankle's twisted. Just a minute!"

And there he was, hobbling out of the shadows, walking with an exaggerated limp. Tripp looked even worse than when he was kidnapped, if such a thing was possible. His muddy, wet fatigues were now torn in several places, showing bloody scratches on the flesh beneath. Tripp's hair stood up in spikes, stiffened by mud or something else. His haggard face had paled beneath his year-round tan. Blood caked his nostrils, and his cheeks were daubed with muck.

The sentries did not instantly relax. They kept their guard up, waiting for another to emerge from hiding, perhaps still using Tripp as a shield. Thomas felt their tension, shared it with them, holding steady with his weapon.

"I'm alone," Tripp said, as if reading their minds. "I broke away from him a few miles out. Jumped in a goddamned river and it carried me downstream. If you had crocodiles, they'd be digesting me by now."

"At ease," Thomas commanded, and the riflemen reluctantly obeyed. Tripp closed the gap between them, lurching wearily along, waving off the salute Thomas offered. "How may I help you, sir?"

"I need a shower, hot. Something to eat, ditto. While I get squared away, you need to turn out every man and weapon we've got left in camp. Prepare to go after that bastard as soon as I'm cleaned up and ready to go."

"You wish to chase him now?" Thomas could not hide his surprise.

"Chase him? Hell, no! I want to skin the prick alive and nail his hide to the nearest tree. Slick bastard thinks he's got the best of me, he needs to think again. His fucking nightmare ends when I say so!"

SOME OF THE SENTRIES were bolder than others. Bolan was counting on that, moving through the forest slowly, quietly, advancing step by silent step. The weapon in his hand was Eduardo's switchblade knife, snapped open long before he reached the camp to avoid any telltale sound that might betray him.

His reunion with Johnny and Ross had been brief. An introduction to Robert Grant and a long drink from his brother's canteen, and Bolan had sketched out his plan in two minutes flat. Johnny and Ross were skeptical, he saw it in their eyes, but neither offered any opposition to the scheme. They knew he had to try it, and both came along for the ride.

Bolan sent Robert Grant to prepare his people in case the plan failed. He took some convincing but the Executioner promised Grant that leading Johnny and Ross to the rebel camp, and their reunion with Bolan, would avenge his brother's death. And if Bolan failed, Grant was free to continue the fight.

Johnny and Ross were on station in the forest even now, waiting for Bolan to complete the first step in his plan. He needed something better than the pistols he was carrying, in order to assault the rebel camp. Since Ross and Johnny carried no spare weapons, Bolan had decided to accept one from his enemies on loan and make the most of it.

The sentry he was stalking stood thirty yards beyond the camp's western perimeter. The man was on his own, well out of sight from camp, and Bolan didn't know if he'd been stationed there on purpose, or if he'd broken discipline and simply wandered off. In either case, the lookout was about to get a rude surprise.

Bolan approached from the sentry's blind side, moving in a slow-motion crouch that strained the muscles of his calves and thighs until they burned. He placed each foot precisely, weighed each step before committing his weight to the move, keeping his left arm ready to clutch and hold his target, while the right was coiled against his side.

Closer.

The sentry shifted, cleared his throat. Bolan froze, prepared to rush him if the gunman turned, uncertain whether he could close the gap and make the kill before his adversary fired his M-16. The warning to his comrades would be bad enough; a close-range hit from one or more of those 5.56 mm tumbling projectiles could stop Bolan dead in his tracks.

The lookout settled, scratched his crotch, but didn't turn. Bolan gave him another moment, conscious of the time slipping away, his friends already at their posts and waiting for his signal. They hadn't synchronized watches, since Bolan had none and he couldn't predict exactly how long it would take him to find and disarm a lone sentry. Johnny and Ross were waiting for Bolan to kick off the party, and they would keep waiting until he gave the signal—or until the enemy discovered them and they had no choice but to fight.

Bolan covered the last ten feet in a near-silent rush. He ignored the sentry's rifle for the moment, clamped a hand across the young man's mouth and gave his head a brutal twist. At the same time, he rammed the switchblade's tip into the narrow space between his target's skull and first cervical vertebrae, lunging for depth, twisting and worrying the blade.

The sentry went stiff in Bolan's grasp, convulsing, his rifle tumbling from spastic fingers to land at his feet. A final shudder rippled through the dying soldier's body, and then he went limp and became deadweight in Bolan's arms.

The Executioner stepped aside, letting him fall. He wiped the knife and closed it, stowed it in his pocket, then retrieved the soldier's M-16. Another moment passed while Bolan worked the bandolier of spare mags off the body and slipped the canvas strap over his head and left shoulder. Finally, he pulled the rifle's magazine, confirmed a full load, and jacked a round into the chamber.

He turned back to the camp and moved up to the firing line.

THE SHOWER HAD REFRESHED Tripp slightly, though the hottest water couldn't leech bone-deep exhaustion from his body. What he really needed was a good eight hours of sleep, but that was out of the question. There'd be no rest for anyone in camp until Tripp had recovered his escaped prisoner and determined that no further threat to their plans yet remained.

It was a tall order, granted, but the merc could not afford to cut himself any slack. In the past eighteen hours, he'd survived two brushes with death and Tripp had no confidence that he would make it through a third.

Preemptive action was the key, if any time remained.

And if it was too late, he'd have a running head start on whomever the cartel sent in to replace him.

But where would he run?

That planning was for later. Tripp finished dressing in a new set of fatigues, tied his boots, strapped on his combat webbing and removed an M-16 rifle from the rack of four on his wall. The weapon was loaded and ready. All Tripp had to do was cock it, set the safety, and he was ready to go.

His team was waiting for him in the center of the camp. Captain Thomas had reluctantly chosen ten men from the thirty remaining, including the camp's two best trackers. If the prisoner had left them any trail at all, those two—

Deckard and Smythe—should be able to find it. Tripp knew they had to start looking at the point where he'd taken his swan dive and powered downstream. If they couldn't find the quarry's tracks there, he'd fall back on Plan B—as in run for your life.

The river had saved him—and it had nearly killed him, too. Tripp had been battered by rocks and dead logs as the current swept him along, going under several times when he was stunned and barely conscious. Finally, he'd grabbed one of the larger logs and dragged himself out of the water's grip. Much more, and Tripp believed he would have drowned, his body carried on downstream until it reached the sea.

But now the shoe was on the other foot and it was payback time. He still wanted a chance to grill his former prisoner, but Tripp would settle for a quick, clean kill if that was the best he could do. One decent shot, in fact, would make his day.

But first he had to find the bastard.

Standing before the team, he scanned their faces, then addressed them. "You men all know who we're after. You were watching when he took me out of here, after he shot your friends. I want you to remember them and help me bring him back—alive, if possible. If not, I'll settle for his head."

A couple of them smiled at that, the others just looked nervous.

"Now, before we start, there is a possibility the man we're after may have allies on the island. I was looking for them yesterday when we ran into regulars outside Johnstown. It isn't likely that he'll find them wandering around the forest, but you've been advised. Stay sharp and be—"

Alert.

The word was on Tripp's tongue and halfway past his lips when an explosion rocked the camp. Tripp ducked, instinctively, the other men likewise. One of them yelped as shrapnel stung him, reaching back to grab his rear.

"Grenade!" someone called out, too late.

Tripp saw smoke rising from the former prison hut, and he was moving in that direction, calling for the other troops to follow him, when a second blast ripped through his quarters, twenty yards behind him.

Incredulous, he gripped his rifle, cold eyes flicking back and forth between the damaged buildings. Fucking hand grenades. That meant the enemy was sitting less than a hundred yards into the woods.

"Get on your battle stations!" Tripp commanded, shouting to the camp at large. "Move it! Right now!"

JOHNNY PALMED his second frag grenade a moment after Ross's first exploded in the camp. He'd hit the prison hut to start with, now he yanked another pin and lobbed his lethal egg as far as he could manage toward the center of the camp, where men were scattering on orders to assume their battle stations. There was no real hope of nailing Garrett Tripp from where he stood, but maybe he could raise a little hell.

Johnny was moving by the time his second charge exploded, ready with his CAR-15 as rebels rushed toward the perimeter in an uneven skirmish line. Aside from Tripp, there seemed to be no other mercenaries in the camp. Johnny assumed there had to be others somewhere on the island, but he didn't know their numbers or their distribution. There were clearly other rebel camps located somewhere in the countryside, perhaps with other men like Tripp in charge. Johnny could only hope that none of them were close enough to reinforce this one.

Which brought him to communications and his brother's

order to destroy all outside links if possible. There seemed to be no commo hut, and Johnny guessed that any radio equipment the guerrillas had in camp would be located in one of the officer's quarters. Ross had already blasted the hut from which Tripp had emerged moments earlier. All that remained was for Johnny to locate the black captain's digs, choosing from two undamaged huts of equal size.

When in doubt, take 'em out.

As luck would have it, both buildings stood within twenty yards of Johnny's position, but he couldn't reach either until he'd dealt with the half-dozen guerrillas advancing in his general direction. He scuttled to the cover of a giant, mossy log and braced his weapon on the makeshift rest.

He started with the soldier nearest to his hiding place, banking on that one to react more swiftly when he started firing. With the carbine set for 3-round bursts, he locked sights on the runner's chest and stroked the trigger once, watching his target reel and stumble as the manglers ripped into his chest.

The second nearest of the five survivors didn't know his comrade had been shot when Johnny swiveled, found his mark and fired another burst from thirty yards. It wasn't quite as clean this time, a little low, but it was good enough to stop the gut-shot soldier in his tracks and put him down.

There was no time for mercy rounds until he'd worked his way along the line, and Johnny pivoted without delay to find his third target. The others had a sense of what was happening by then, and number three was running in a zigzag pattern that proved totally predictable. Johnny was ready when he zigged and pulled the trigger when he zagged, leaving the clever rebel with a stunned expression on his dying face.

And that left three.

All of the rest were firing now, though only one of them

appeared to know where Johnny was, and even his fire wasn't on the mark. Fear and the rush of movement spoiled their aim. Johnny was busy tracking them, trying to nail all three before they found cover, but he was running out of time.

He broke the pattern with a sweep to his far left, seeking the shooter farthest from his hiding place. His logic was impeccable: that soldier was nearest to cover and one of the huts Johnny wanted to raze, which made him a threat if he had time to gather his wits and acquire a target. The other two, while closer to Johnny, were farther from adequate cover right now, while their hasty shots were flying high and wide.

He found the runner, led him by six feet or so and fired another burst. It was peculiar when the man ran into Johnny's bullets, jerking through an awkward little pirouette as if someone had jerked a hidden string to make him spin.

Two left, and when he spotted them again, Johnny discovered that they'd made a critical mistake. Instead of separating, seeking cover individually, they had turned as one to charge at his position, firing from the hip as they advanced. It was a bold but foolish move, an all-or-nothing kind of play that ought to be reserved for hopeless situations.

Johnny wasn't sure their situation had been hopeless seconds earlier, but now it was.

He met them with a head-on double burst, two trigger strokes that dumped them on the ground together in a tangled mess of arms and legs. There'd been no time for them to register surprise or recognize the fatal error they'd made.

With twelve rounds left inside his magazine, Johnny leaped clear of cover and rushed toward the nearer of his unprotected targets. There was no one at the door to stop him when he kicked it in, then charged inside.

DESPITE THE CHAOS all around him, Captain Thomas hadn't fired a shot. He clutched his rifle tightly, fingers aching from his grip's ferocity, but Thomas had been trained to fire only when there were targets. Thus far, he'd seen nothing but the evidence of enemies around him: the grenade explosions, soldiers dropping to the ground with bloody wounds, but Thomas couldn't have pointed out those enemies to save his own life.

It might yet come to that, Thomas knew. He fought an urge to flee the camp and race blindly through the forest like a madman until he was miles from the scene and at last safe from harm. It was an impulse every soldier felt sometime, Thomas believed, but most were able to control it. Could his dedication to the cause help him to stay the course?

THE BASTARDS NEARLY got her in the mess tent. Ross was moving in, watching for shooters, thinking she could blow the propane stove and draw a number of them off that way, when two guerrillas leaped from hiding and attacked her. One of them, incredibly, was armed with a machete that he swung at Ross's face, attempting to behead her.

She ducked under it, with perhaps a inch to spare, and felt the wide blade graze her hair on top. Acting on pure reflex, she slammed the butt of her assault rifle into the rebel's forward knee and heard him howl in pain. Ross's upstroke blocked him from delivering a backhand slash across her shoulder, and she whipped the muzzle hard into his twisted face. The impact staggered him and left her free to face her second adversary for a moment.

Just in time, she saw, as this one had an old blue-steel revolver gripped in both hands, aiming at her face. Ross dropped and fired as part of the same motion, stitching him with half a dozen rounds from groin to throat. The dead man still got off one shot, and Ross heard someone squeal behind her. She turned in time to see the guy with the machete clutching at the left side of his head. It seemed to be a graze, maybe his ear. Ross didn't question it, just fired a round into his wailing mouth and shut him up for good.

She turned back to the stove before another interruption could distract her. It was fairly small, considering the troops it fed three times a day. The propane tank was short and fat, about the size of an overweight fire hydrant. Ross had considered using a grenade to set it off, but she'd dismissed that means as overkill. A bullet ought to do the trick, she thought, as long as she was safely out of range.

How far was that?

She didn't have a clue, but thirty feet seemed reasonable. Backing up another ten for caution's sake, glancing about to check for snipers on her flank, she crouched, lined up her shot and sped a bullet on its way toward impact with the tank.

The force of the blast surprised her. She was pitched backward with a gust of flame and superheated air that singed her eyebrows to the roots and left her gasping. The report was deafening, its shock wave rippling through the camp, but the most startling thing about it was the way a fragment of the ruptured tank took flight, riding a yellow tail of fire straight up, beyond the treetops, like a rocket bound for outer space.

Ross didn't see it land, though logic told her gravity had to reassert itself at some point. She was on her feet again before the echoes of the blast had dissipated, seeking other targets on the battlefield.

Some of the tents were burning now, touched off by the propane explosion, crumpling as if made of paper while the flames devoured them. They were unoccupied, as far as she could tell—no safety under canvas when the bullets started flying—but their immolation added more confusion to the scene and set the rebels running every which way, seemingly without purpose.

Ross saw no one she recognized among the runners, either from her party or the mug shots she had reviewed. No Garrett Tripp, no one from the cartel. She hadn't really expected to find the men in charge camped out here in the forest, but it struck her as a disappointment, always dealing with the small-fry while the big fish slipped away.

The shot was a surprise. It struck Ross in the back, below her shoulder blade, and exited beneath her breast. Falling, she felt a sense of fullness in her chest and knew the lung was perforated, maybe filling with blood. The grim phrase *sucking chest wound* came to mind, but she was on the ground then, clutching at her weapon, desperate not to lose it.

As her consciousness began to fade, Ross thought this had to be how it felt to die.

BOLAN DROPPED THE EMPTY magazine from his M-16 and replaced it on the run with a fresh one. No sooner had he jacked a round into the chamber than a target sprang up in his path, howling a battle cry and brandishing a vintage M-14 assault rifle.

Bolan didn't wait to see if the guerrilla was proficient with his weapon. A short burst of 5.56 mm shredders took off the gunman's face and dumped his twitching body on the ground.

One more for the worms, and he still hadn't found the target he sought.

During his hike back to the camp with his companions, Bolan had considered the possibility that he might never see Tripp again. The jungle might have finished him, or Tripp could have decided to keep on running, make his way off the island and look for a safe place to hide. That worry had dissolved when Bolan reached the rebel camp and saw his captor freshly showered, limping as he rallied troops to mount another jungle sweep.

It had been tempting to kill Tripp with his first shot, but Bolan still wanted the mercenary alive, to help him find the cartel leaders and unravel any secrets that remained about their means and motives. Accordingly, he'd used the frag grenade borrowed from his brother to destroy the hut where he'd been caged—and thus began the rebel camp's last battle. Tripp had taken swift advantage of the chaos, though, and dropped from sight.

Had he escaped again?

It was a possibility Bolan acknowledged, but he wouldn't know until they'd swept the camp and peered into every dead face they could find. If Tripp was not among them, it would mean he'd wriggled out of yet another trap.

And when would Bolan have another chance at him?

The camp's motor pool consisted of a dozen mismatched bicycles, probably stolen from surrounding villages, chained together on the east side of the compound. Bolan found two rebels grappling with the chain, apparently intent on bailing out, but they were baffled by the cheap combination locks, reduced to shaking the bikes of their choice in a frenzy of frustration.

"Going somewhere?" Bolan asked them, and the startled pair swung to face him, both men reaching for the weapons they had laid aside.

"You'll never make it," Bolan warned them, holding steady with his M-16. They hesitated, staring, as he said, "Point me to Garrett Tripp and you can ride away—unarmed, that is. The lock will be my treat."

The rebels shared a glance and something passed between them. Bolan couldn't read it in their eyes, but there was no mistaking their intention as they lunged in opposite directions for their rifles, gambling that Bolan couldn't drop them both before one of them took him down.

They were mistaken.

Bolan shot the soldier on his left, a clean hit to the temple, and the man was dead before he fell across his useless weapon. To Bolan's right, the second shooter may have guessed his friend was gone, but stopping once he had begun the move was not an option. He had reached his rifle and was lifting it when Bolan triggered two quick shots at point-blank range and sent a fist-sized fragment of the rebel's skull sailing through space.

"Who's next?" he asked the smoky air, but no one answered. Bolan kept on moving through the camp that had become a killing ground, glancing at corpses on the way. So far, he'd found no white faces among them. Garrett Tripp was either still alive, or Bolan simply hadn't found his body yet.

Whichever was the case, he had to remedy the situation soon. Despite his team's best efforts, rebel reinforcements might be on the way—or army regulars, if they were prowling in the neighborhood, searching for enemies. He'd heard about the other clash from Johnny and he had no yen to mix it up with Isla de Victoria's defenders.

Not today, at any rate.

Given the choice, he'd take it one war at a time, and this one wasn't over yet.

Not while the men who'd caged and tried to kill him were alive.

The Executioner moved on through smoke and flame in search of human prey.

12

Garrett Tripp lay beside the smoking rubble of a blasted hut and wondered how in hell he could get out of there.

The words *in hell* reverberated in his mind with a disturbing resonance. He'd seen enough of combat, as a regular and mercenary, to believe he'd seen it all—before this relatively simple mission blew up in his face. The fight for Isla de Victoria had been protracted, but the tide was running in his favor, flowing toward a resolution that would please his many employers, when it suddenly changed without warning and everything began to fall apart.

And Tripp had been running in place ever since, expending maximum effort for minimum gains.

Strike that: There'd been *no* gains in the past two weeks, only losses. Even his coup with the prisoner—Borodin's really, but who was keeping score these days?—had gone sour in the end, nearly claiming his life when the tables were turned. Tripp had been ready to pursue it, do his utmost to reclaim his reputation, but here he was again, belly down in the mud with bullets flying overhead.

Some operations were cursed from the get-go, it seemed. Tripp wasn't superstitious, by any means; he trusted no power greater than firepower. But sometimes a mission simply went wrong, beyond redemption.

Sometimes it went FUBAR.

And when that happened, smart soldiers did what they could to survive.

It had been one thing, when he wore his country's uniform and swore an oath to sacrifice himself, if need be, to satisfy the whim of deskbound politicians in Washington. The mercenary game was played by different rules. He was a businessman whose business happened to include mayhem, the toppling of governments and sudden death. Commitment to a contract or employer had its limitations, though.

Tripp had agreed to risk his life, not flush it down the toilet on a job where he was guaranteed to fail. If the cartel wanted suicide commandos, he could point them to any number of Middle Eastern groups whose members thought nothing of killing themselves for a cause. Tripp could put them in touch, and the gang could do lunch.

All he asked for his trouble was a healthy finder's fee.

Three rebels ran past him, boots churning the mud. If they saw or recognized Tripp where he lay, they gave no indication of it. They were twenty paces past him when a bullet struck the middle runner and he went down on his face.

A sniper round, or careless friendly fire?

Tripp couldn't say, but it was getting thick out there. Every mother's son with a weapon was firing at something—or at nothing, hoping for a lucky score. Tripp hadn't glimpsed the enemy so far, but something told him they were looking for the man who'd held him hostage only hours earlier. The prisoner who'd turned the game around on Tripp and nearly killed him.

The same man who...

Hell, no. It couldn't be!

Could it?

He was thinking the bastard wouldn't have the nerve to come back here, where he'd been caged and nearly killed, but Tripp knew that was wrong. It was exactly what the guy would do, given half a chance.

Tripp's eyes became more focused, sweeping the camp again with a special target in mind. He sought the nameless enemy who'd been within his grasp, then slipped away. The soldier who'd humiliated Tripp in front of his men and who would certainly come back to kill him if he could.

Tripp started edging backward, worried that a sudden move would draw the hunters to him, or make one of his own men mistake him for an enemy. Slowly, cautiously, Tripp worked his way around the rubble pile until he had a clear view of the tree line, eighty yards away.

So close, and yet so far.

Between him and the trees, another demolished hut would offer cover at the halfway point. If he could get that far without a bullet screaming through the smoke to find him, Tripp could rest, regain his nerve, get ready for the final rush.

No problem, he decided. Forty yards. A piece of cake.

At last, with grim determination, he began to crawl across the open killing ground.

JOHNNY WAS READY when the rebels made their move. Three of them rushed him in a bid that smacked of desperation, and he welcomed it, stretched out behind a bullet-punctured storage shed.

He took the point man first, clipping his legs on the run, then sealing the kill with a quick double tap as the target went down. A shudder rippled through the dying rebel's body, but

Johnny didn't see it. He had moved on by that time, tracking his other targets on the field.

Dropping the middle man had left a gap between the others and encouraged them to separate. They recognized their danger but pressed forward, although veering off on different paths. Both knew approximately where he was and they were fairly decent shots, which made it difficult for Johnny to choose his second mark.

Mechanics made the decisions. It was easier to swivel leftward, optimizing leverage and taking care of business with a twelve-inch sweep that translated to some twenty feet on the receiving end. He led the target by a fraction, fired a short burst and let his adversary run into the bullets on a dead collision course.

He marked his target's fall in his peripheral vision, moving on to the next threat in line.

The third guerrilla was fast, but he lost some accuracy with his speed, bullets fanning the air and drilling the walls above Johnny's head. It was a natural mistake, quite common in battle, but the gods of war were unforgiving.

Johnny held his aim, ignored the storm of fire passing above him, and squeezed off a short burst at his target from a range of fifteen yards. Johnny saw his bullets hit, an inch or two above the target's belt buckle, jolting the man off-stride and spinning him halfway around before he fell. The rebel went down firing, burning half a magazine on nothing by the time he hit the deck.

How many left?

Johnny didn't have a clue, although the field was thinning out from where he lay, with fewer targets on the move. Their purpose was twofold, to raze the rebel camp and locate Garrett Tripp. They'd made a fair start on the first objective,

Johnny reckoned, but he hadn't caught a glimpse of Tripp since Mack's grenade had kicked off the party and chaos descended upon the compound.

I should've tracked him, Johnny thought, but it was like a shell game or a round of Three-Card Monty. The point of focus could be lost in nothing flat, and once a player lost it, it might never be regained. When gambling on the street, of course, the only things at stake were pride and money. On a battlefield, the stakes were life or death.

They had to find Tripp. But how?

The merc wasn't invisible. He couldn't violate the laws of physics. Thus, if Johnny couldn't see him at the moment it meant one of two things. Either some obstacle stood between them, or Tripp had fled into the forest.

If Tripp was gone, Johnny acknowledged, there was nothing he could do about it. But if Tripp was hiding in the camp, he could be found. It might take time, and it would be a risky game of hide-and-seek, but it was possible.

Cursing his own determination, Johnny set off crawling from his shelter to the next building, already blasted by a frag grenade.

He had to start somewhere.

And there was no time better than right now.

THE REBELS WERE tenacious, Bolan had to give them that. A few had run away into the forest, but most of them stood their ground, fighting as if the camp was home. He didn't know if they were dedicated to the cause they'd chosen, or if they had nowhere else to go, but it was not his job to analyze the opposition in the middle of a firefight.

He only had to take them out.

Bolan gave them credit for making him work at it. They

weren't exactly the ragtag band of peasants he'd expected. They'd been adequately trained, but Bolan had a sense that they were used to fighting slackers, maybe local army regulars who didn't look beyond survival and their next paycheck when they were on the firing line. It was a different kind of war when the opponent vowed to either win or die.

Bolan edged around the corner of a bullet-riddled hut, checking before he made the move. A dead man lay beside the building, slack and nearly faceless from a head shot. He'd been one of Tripp's, but Bolan couldn't say who'd done the shooting. In the present atmosphere, it could've been Johnny, Ross, or a case of friendly fire. As long as he was down and out, it made no difference to the Executioner.

Bolan stepped around the body, moving toward the southeast corner of the small building. Sporadic fire still rattled on from several points around the camp, but it was waning. Bolan didn't know if he should credit thinning numbers for the change, or if his enemies were simply calming down a bit, choosing their targets more selectively. He hoped it was the former, but—

A young guerrilla suddenly appeared in front of Bolan, seeking shelter from the firestorm. When his eyes first locked on Bolan's face, they bulged, as if he'd seen a ghost. Bolan assumed the young soldier had been among the group that watched him escape with Tripp some hours earlier. In any case, the momentary hesitation sealed his fate, as Bolan fired a single shot into his chest from seven feet and put him down.

Bolan ignored the latest twitching corpse and reached the corner that had been his destination when the dead man interrupted him. The new vantage point let him scan one-third of the camp without great risk from snipers. He used the moment to search for his comrades and caught a fleeting glimpse of Johnny on the far side of the compound, ducking out of sight behind an open shed. There was no sign of Ross, and none of Tripp, the only member of the home team Bolan hoped to take alive. It might be futile, but he still had questions begging answers, still required more information if he meant to vanquish the cartel directing Maxwell Reed.

Unwilling and unable to give up the search, he drew a deep breath, held it for a moment while his own pulse hammered in his ears, then let it go and stepped into the open killing zone.

THE HUNT HAD NOT GONE well for Captain Bertram Thomas. He had found no enemies to kill, but rather saw his own men dying all around him, killed by adversaries he could not pin down or by their own comrades. The captain wished that he could slap and shake each surviving soldier in the camp, commanding them to hold their fire until a clear-cut target was acquired, then make the first shot count.

But it was hopeless now.

He saw that in the faces of the young men still alive and prowling through the camp. Panic had overpowered and eradicated discipline. Thomas suspected some had fled the camp already; others surely would before much longer, if they could escape the slaughterhouse alive. His own thoughts focused more upon self-preservation than on defeating his unknown and seemingly invisible opponents.

And that meant getting out.

As luck would have it, he was nearly in the middle of the camp, surrounded on all sides by carnage and gunfire. A brief glance at his options seemed to indicate no one direction safer than the others, no path likely to deliver him unscathed into the woods. It was a miracle, thought Thomas, that he hadn't yet been wounded. He could not expect that luck to hold, with enemies still unidentified in camp and rebel targets thinning by the moment.

A man of action when he had to be, the captain flipped a mental coin and thereby chose to exit on the west. If he had stopped to think about it further, Thomas might have told himself the nearest coastline lay in that direction, and perhaps he could obtain a boat, leave Isla de Victoria and its demented politics behind forever.

But to escape the island, he had to first escape the camp.

Thomas began his move toward the perimeter, a thing of fits and starts, ducking and dodging, meeting scattered troops along the way and barking orders to divert them, sending them in search of enemies he couldn't see. The last thing Thomas needed was a band of stragglers following him, leaving a trail to show the enemy which way he'd gone.

Thomas was halfway to his destination, almost willing to allow himself a taint of optimism, when he saw a figure dressed in camouflage fatigues emerging from the shadow of a barracks hut. The captain froze, clutching his rifle so tightly that his fingers ached and muscles started twitching in his arms.

Was this the enemy?

He squinted through a drifting pall of smoke and verified that the tiger-stripe camouflage pattern matched nothing worn by his men. Further, the lurker's skin was white beneath a layer of smeared war paint, the hair some muted reddish shade. He hesitated for a second longer, thinking maybe it was one of Tripp's hired killers, then remembered that the last mercenary in camp had been the bull-necked Barry Joslin, dead and gone.

It struck Thomas that the stranger was moving curiously, hobbling rather than sneaking, pausing after half a dozen steps to slump against the barracks wall and use it for support. He didn't understand at first, until a glint of scarlet on the green-and-brown-striped tunic clarified the matter for him.

Wounded.

Someone else had done the hard work for him, but presumably had not survived to claim the prize. So much the better, Thomas thought. Why should some private who most likely scored a lucky shot by accident get credit for the kill?

Smiling for the first time in days—or was it weeks?—Thomas held steady with his rifle, framed the stationary target in his sights and fired.

YOU NEVER HEAR the shot that kills you.

Keely Ross couldn't remember where or when she'd first heard that old saying, but she wished that she could find whoever said it, grab him by his wattled throat and tell him he was wrong.

Ross couldn't say with any certainty which of the many shots she'd heard today had pierced her torso, leaving her to choke on her own blood, but she was living proof—for a few minutes yet—that the old chestnut ought to be retired.

After the stunning impact and the first raw flush of panic, Ross had recovered enough to rip a piece of fabric from her cammo shirt and plug the wound beneath her breast. It hurt like hell, and there was nothing she could do about the entrance wound in her back, but it was slightly easier to draw breath now, without a sense that she was thrashing underwater, on the verge of drowning.

Still, she knew it was a respite, nothing more. Ross needed surgery, and soon, if she was going to survive. But there was no MASH unit standing by with trauma surgeons at the ready, no evacuation flight to speed her from the jungle to an operating room. The sheer futility of Ross's situation might have made her laugh, if she could draw a steady breath.

Die laughing, she thought, and coughed a gout of crimson down her chin.

Ross took two halting steps before a giant fist struck her midsection, slamming her back against the barracks wall. Her legs buckled, pain flaring from waist to knees, and again she heard the echo of automatic fire. She smelled sawdust amid the gunsmoke where bullets had drilled the wall on either side of her.

Ross lay huddled on the ground, uncertain what had happened to her CAR-15. Her pistol was wedged underneath her, the sharp dig at her side barely felt in competition with her injuries. Amazingly the freshest wounds were going numb already, which she took to be a bad sign, from the standpoint of survival.

Numb is never good, she thought, unless you're in a dentist's chair.

Numb meant she had some kind of massive neural damage, or maybe she was just bleeding out so swiftly that her body had already started shutting down. Forget about that MASH unit, that medevac chopper. Has anyone got a spare body bag?

Ross saw the man who'd killed her approaching. She had a weird upside-down-and-sideways view of his legs and the rifle he carried. It took another endless moment for his face to fill her field of vision. He was staring at her curiously, like he'd never seen—

"A woman?" he muttered. Then louder, addressing himself to Ross directly. "You're a *woman?* What does this mean?"

She forced a crooked, bloody smile. "Don't let it worry you, asshole."

"Impossible!" The shooter straightened and looked around, as if afraid someone would find him there. Ross drew another breath and found, to her immense displeasure, that the fall had dislodged the crude plug from her chest wound. If she didn't bleed to death within the next few moments, she would—

The soldier crouched beside her, frowning like a scientist who couldn't make sense of what he was seeing through his microscope. Bracing the assault rifle across his knees, he reached out with one hand to pinch Ross's breast. A confirmation of the absurd.

"A woman. Impossible."

She felt him fumbling at the buttons of her shirt, undoing them. A sudden rush of outrage helped her find the Ka-Bar knife strapped to her combat webbing, draw it and plunge the blade into her killer's plump thigh. With a feral snarl, she twisted the blade, scraping bone, shearing muscle. Withdrawing it as the rebel fell over backward, Ross saw a bright jet of arterial blood chase the blade.

"Grope that," she told the stranger, as he tried in vain to stop the pulse of life escaping from his ravaged leg. Ross had a sudden urge to laugh, but lacked the breath required to follow through. Instead, she drove her knife into the weeping man's other leg.

His screaming followed her into the dark.

WE'RE ALMOST THERE, Garrett Tripp thought.

The *we* in question was Tripp and three guerrillas he'd collected as he made his way out of the camp. They'd asked where he was going, and instead of shooting them—his first instinct, an option he was keeping open for the future—Tripp had told them it was time to split. He'd regroup with the men of Delta Camp and return to punish the invaders properly. Did any of them wish to join him?

Goddamn right, they did.

The thought had come to Tripp belatedly, but not too late. There was a chance that he'd encounter other adversaries in the forest, and it wouldn't hurt to have a few more guns along for backup. He could always ditch them later, making sure they weren't alive to finger his escape route, but for now they still had value of a sort.

If they were ambushed on the trail, for instance, he could slip away and leave his soldiers to amuse the enemy.

If they could just get out of camp alive.

The fighting had begun to wane, but Tripp had no interest in lingering to see which side emerged victorious. Even if Thomas and the others won the day, Tripp's employers would still blame him for losing the prisoner, the camp and thirty-odd soldiers.

It was a no-win situation, and Tripp was fresh out of second chances.

It was definitely time to cut and run.

Of course, it galled Tripp that he'd never know who had defeated him, who'd smeared his name forever in the mercenary line. When he was safe and out of reach, perhaps he could investigate the matter on his own, discreetly, without drawing any of his ex-employers to his hiding place.

Or maybe it was better, just this once, to forget about the whole damned thing and be grateful for getting out alive.

You aren't out yet, he reminded himself, as a new burst of firing erupted from somewhere near the center of the camp. Moments later, as his small squad approached the perimeter, Tripp heard high-pitched, incoherent cries of mortal pain.

Better him than me, Tripp concluded.

A few more yards, and they could start to flee in earnest, covered by the jungle all the way to—where? Tripp wasn't clear on destinations yet. His focus was on getting out, away from where each moment tempted Death to find him and present a bill long overdue.

But not this day, with any luck at all.

They crept past dead and wounded men, ignoring both. Tripp's followers knew well enough that it would cost their lives to tarry here. Self-preservation was the instinct driving them; their talk of payback, getting even, was a masquerade, a means of saving face with Tripp and with themselves.

They wanted out. Whatever else they managed, later, would be frosting on the cake.

Another twenty yards to go. Tripp focused on the tree line that was everything he treasured now. It was concealment and security, release and resurrection.

If he lived that long.

A shape came at them from the smoky shadows, reaching out. Tripp nearly shot the man before he recognized one of his own guerrillas.

"Take me with you!" the private cried. "Please, sir!"

"Where's your weapon?" Tripp demanded, bitter at the thought of wasting precious time.

The rebel glanced down at his hands and seemed surprised to find them empty. "Sir, I...I don't know."

"Jesus. All right, then. Just be quiet and—"

The private's eyes bulged with the impact of a bullet tearing through his skull. Blood and pale tissue spattered Tripp's face. He recoiled as the dead man pitched forward, dropping like a scarecrow made of cloth and moldy straw.

"Run for it!" Tripp commanded, and he sprinted for the trees without a backward glance.

If you bastards want to kill me, said the urgent voice inside his head, you'll have to catch me first!

BOLAN FIRED AGAIN, too quickly, and saw one of the rebels stagger, clutching at his shoulder. Tripp was off and running then, a shadow at the tree line, fading out of sight. The others followed him while Bolan stood and watched them go.

He turned and scanned the compound, looking for Johnny and Ross. There'd been no third headset available this time, and Bolan had declined when Ross offered hers on the trail. Now he was torn between the danger of losing Tripp again and the shame of leaving his comrades behind on the field, without telling them where he had gone.

Seething, Bolan retraced his steps into the killing ground. Pure chance had given him a glimpse of Tripp on the perimeter, and he'd be after the fugitives now if he was working alone, but he couldn't leave Johnny and Ross. Not here. Not when they'd risked their lives repeatedly to free him from captivity.

Beyond the call of common blood, there was a debt the Executioner could not ignore.

He shot two rebels when they tried to intercept him, barely pausing as they sprawled across his path. Blood everywhere, with the smell of death and smoke in his nostrils, but it was nothing new to Bolan.

In fact, it felt like coming home.

He found Johnny kneeling in the shadow of a barracks hut, with Ross laid out before him. Off to Johnny's right, a rebel wearing captain's bars had done a messy job of bleeding out through leg wounds, and the Ka-Bar knife protruding from the guy's right calf told Bolan what had happened.

"Johnny?"

"I was too late, Mack. Too late."

"There's nothing that you could've done," he told his brother.

"She took the bastard with her, anyway."

"That's something." Bolan knew he had to break the mood, the moment, so he said, "I just saw Tripp. He's bugging out. I have to follow him."

"She can't come with us."

"No."

"These sons of bitches," Johnny said. "You don't know what they'll do."

Bolan listened for gunfire and heard none. He swept the compound for movement and saw none but the feeble twitching of the fallen.

"I believe they're done," he told Johnny.

Johnny stood. "All right. Let's finish it. I'll come back later if I can."

"We'll both come back."

Johnny removed his rifle's magazine, checked it and put it back. "Which way?"

They left Ross where she was, Bolan hoping he could make good on the promise to return. Nothing was certain, but at least they had a fighting chance to finish it.

No, that was wrong.

Tripp wasn't the ultimate target; he was simply a means to an end. His death would bring closure of a sort, but first they needed him to talk, if that could be arranged.

And if it couldn't? Then, what?

We'll make do, the Executioner promised himself.

It wasn't over yet, but they were closer than they'd been since the beginning.

Bolan was tired of jungle, tired of hiking through the mud,

while ferns and vines and branches slowed him. He'd had enough of hunting men on unfamiliar ground, and having them hunt him. He'd seen the inside of a cage and vowed it wouldn't happen twice. There was another debt attached to that, aside from what he owed to Garrett Tripp, but that was somewhere down the road.

Right now, the road stretched into trees and shadows, leading eastward.

Bolan followed it, with Johnny on his heels.

13

Johnny wasn't sure where they were headed, and he didn't really care. The sight of Keely Ross, lying dead in the rebel camp, had stunned him as he thought no scene of death or tragedy could ever do again. He'd thought that he had seen it all and run a gamut of emotions that had immunized him to the shocks of life and battle in the kill zone for all time.

But he'd been wrong.

Johnny had blocked himself from thinking words like "love" and "future" in his time with Ross, and in his heart of hearts, he couldn't swear the instant chemistry between them would have led to anything beyond the confines of their strange association. Still, he felt the sting of losing her as nothing else had stung him since his parents and his sister died by violence, so long ago.

To purge the hurt, he concentrated on the trail, his brother's shape in front of him and the image of Garrett Tripp's face in his gunsights. The idea of clutching Tripp's throat with bare hands pleased him, too, but Johnny knew it was unlikely that they'd come to grips for any kind of hand-to-hand encounter.

Mack wanted Tripp alive, for whatever time it took to wring some answers out of him. That was all right with

Johnny, since he guessed the mercenary would resist and take a beating in the process. Anything that hurt Tripp and made him suffer was okay in Johnny's book.

But when Mack had his answers and was satisfied, the merc would die. That part was carved in stone.

Johnny's watch read ten minutes past noon when they reached a narrow stream and Mack started wading across. Johnny covered him from the bank, half expecting an ambush from the other side. It would be an ideal place to do it, if Tripp was intent on taking them down. Then again, it was possible the mercenary didn't even know they were pursuing him. He had a lead and might not want to spend the time required to cover his rear.

So much the better, then.

Johnny, for his part, paused and listened to the forest now and then, checking to see if he and Mack were being hunted by their enemies. He didn't think there were enough survivors from the rebel camp to manage it—or that they'd care to try— but it was always possible a call for reinforcements got through and others were after them. An alternate long-shot scenario put Tripp in touch with more guerrillas, somewhere up ahead, baiting a lethal trap for anyone who followed him.

Johnny considered that, and then dismissed it from his mind. He'd follow Tripp if Tripp had been accompanied by hundreds, thousands. It might change his final strategy, but Johnny would pursue him, bide his time and ultimately take down the bastard.

For Ross. And for what might have been.

His eyes burned, tearing up, but Johnny passed it off as something in the air. He had no allergies, but what the hell. First time for everything. It couldn't be that he was weeping silently while crouching in a steaming jungle, with a rifle in his hands and murder on his mind.

No way.

Big boys didn't cry.

They killed.

Mack reached the other bank safely and waved Johnny across. The groin-deep water wasn't cold by any means, but it was still a shudder-shock compared to the ambient temperature and humidity. Johnny would have liked to slip beneath the surface, maybe let the current sweep him off, away from consciousness and memory, but that would have to wait.

He had a job to do, and it was waiting somewhere up ahead of him.

Unfinished business with the man responsible for Keely's death, and those who paid his way.

Mack was right. It wouldn't be finished with Tripp. Mercs were expendable, disposable. He'd be replaced before the week was out, and the killing would start all over again, with the same men in charge, the same goals in mind.

Johnny realized he couldn't disable a venomous lizard by clipping its toenails.

He'd have to smash the creature's head.

It was the same principle in this case, but the monster had multiple heads, and they rarely congregated in one place. It sounded like another long, protracted struggle, but he didn't mind.

Johnny reached the bank, slipped once in mud and caught his brother's outstretched hand before he fell. A moment later, he was back on solid ground and following Mack's tall, familiar figure through the trees.

That's how they'd finish it, Johnny thought.

Hand in hand. Facing the bastards side by side or back-to-back, whatever was required. And if one of them fell along the way, the other would finish alone.

Being as close as he would come to peace this bloody day, Johnny blanked out his mind and concentrated on the forest trail.

WE'RE GETTING THERE, Tripp thought. And then the small voice in his head replied, okay, but where the hell is there?

He didn't know and wasn't overly concerned about it at the moment. Progress was what mattered, putting miles between himself and the charnel house of the camp while there was time. Before someone on either side missed him and started sending out patrols.

The wounded man was slowing them. A small round had pierced his shoulder, through and through, with the entry wound behind. Tripp would have left him on the trail, but his companions wouldn't hear of it. Under the circumstances, Tripp had reasoned that it wasn't in his best interest to force a confrontation with the other three, even if one of them was weak and gimpy. He could always shoot them, but he didn't want to make a racket in the woods right now if it could be avoided.

So they blazed a trail more slowly than he would have liked, but truth be told, Tripp's ass was dragging just as much as anyone else's by now. He'd been up all night, tramping around the jungle as a hostage, then back to camp on his own to organize pursuit of his hostage-turned-captor-turned-fugitive. The world had blown up in his face, then, and now he was back on the run, with no clear fix on where that night or tomorrow's sunrise would find him.

Fucking wonderful, he thought. Just marvelous.

It could've been much worse, though.

Tripp could just as easily have been among the dead in camp, and there was no way weary muscles or an aching back compared to that.

Midway through the second hour of their trek, the others called for a rest stop. Tripp didn't argue, taking up the rearguard post on his own initiative and blanking out their conversation as they tended to their wounded friend. Watching the shadows and the trees, he wondered how such men could ever win a war. The answer that came back at him was by pure dumb luck, or not at all.

Either way, the problem was no longer his.

Tripp's companions didn't know it yet, but he wasn't leading them anywhere. He didn't plan on meeting up with troops from Delta Camp or any other rebel base, much less mounting a strike against the enemy who'd nearly killed him three times now.

Tripp's mother hadn't been much to write home about, all things considered, but she hadn't raised a fool.

He'd have to think about disposing of the others, the mechanics of it, when he made his final break. If they were willing to part company and strike out on their own, so be it. If they tried to argue, or insisted on remaining with Tripp, he could settle the argument with his M-16. But he'd have to be crafty about it and make sure they didn't see it coming.

Never give a target an even break.

Tripp counted off five minutes, gave them one to grow on, then walked back to where the others huddled on the trail. "It's time to go," he said.

"Julian is weak from loss of blood," their spokesman replied.

"That's what happens, all right."

"We cannot leave him," said the mouthpiece.

"Can't, or won't?" Tripp challenged.

The two on their feet exchanged glances, both frowning. Tripp eased the safety off his M-16 and hoped they didn't notice.

"He is our friend," the rebel said.

"I understand that and admire it," Tripp replied. "A friend wouldn't want his buddies getting killed or captured because he can't keep up. A soldier understands these things."

"We'll carry him!" the second rebel blurted out.

Tripp shrugged. "It's worth a try. Of course, the men who're chasing us won't be slowed down by anybody riding piggyback."

Wide eyes. "You really think they'll follow us?" the first one asked.

"Think about it," Tripp advised him. "Whether the camp was hit by Halsey's regulars or someone else, they'll want to make it a clean sweep. It won't take long to spot our trail, with Julian all bloody there. We're wasting time, and he's a target painted on our backs. Something to think about."

"But leaving him…"

"A soldier understands these things," Tripp repeated. "Is he a man, or not?"

"Of course!"

"He has the choice then to fight or fly, whatever strikes him as the way to go."

"We leave him with a rifle, then?"

"We could do that," Tripp said. "Why don't you toss a coin to see which one of you goes on unarmed."

They clearly didn't like the sound of that. For his part, wounded Julian was lolling back against a tree trunk, barely conscious.

"How can he defend himself," asked the second rebel, "if he has no gun?"

"The way I've seen it done," Tripp said, "you leave him something nice and quiet, like a knife. That way, he's not so much a threat to anyone who comes along, and they won't gun him down on sight. Maybe he'll just surrender, or surprise them with the knife. Maybe he'll think of something else to do with it."

"I have a knife," the first one said.

"He's weak," the second challenged. "We can't leave him here like this."

"Hey, it's your friend. Your call. Decide what's best, and I'll go on ahead. How's that?"

Tripp turned away without waiting for an answer, pushing on into the trees. He didn't listen for a struggle, rather concentrating on his footsteps, watching out for roots and snakes. The others caught up with him moments later, sweaty, out of breath.

"We talked to him," one said. "He's better now."

Tripp managed to suppress a smile. "That's how it goes, sometimes."

BOLAN HAD SEEN the blood and called Johnny's attention to it where the splotches showed from time to time. It wasn't constant, like a person bleeding out, but he was still surprised to note that Tripp had let the wounded rebel tag along.

"Maybe the others didn't give him any choice," Johnny suggested.

In any case, Bolan was grateful for the late addition to Tripp's team, because a wounded soldier always slowed the others. It was a law of nature. Tripp would choose to ditch the excess baggage soon, Bolan thought, but until then they would take advantage of their quarry's slower pace and make up time.

Bolan hadn't tried to counsel Johnny on his loss, not knowing what it was, precisely, how much had been shared or felt between his brother and the woman. It would be presumptuous of him to speculate, and it would also be a waste of precious time.

For every step they took, the enemy was taking one or two steps in the distance, trying to escape. If Bolan let Tripp slip away this time, he knew that it might be impossible to find his trail again.

And that was unacceptable.

They found the wounded man at 2:13 p.m. He wasn't wounded any more, but rather dead. Someone had slashed his throat from ear to ear, and any hint of suicide had been erased when they forgot to leave the knife behind.

"He slowed them down too much," Johnny said.

"Looks that way. We'll have to bump up the pace."

Bolan searched the dead man's pockets, knowing it was likely futile, but he didn't want to miss the opportunity. Sometimes a soldier carried items that could tell a stranger where he'd been, or where he planned to go.

Nothing.

"Trail markers only, now," he told his brother. "No more blood to show the way."

"Then it's a good thing you're on point. Let's go," Johnny replied.

They went, marching past weariness and into a kind of twilight zone where instinct took over and physical strain ceased to matter. Bolan stayed alert, watching the bare suggestion of a trail for signs and any indication of a trap ahead, but that part of his mind seemed detached from his body, refusing to acknowledge scrapes or bruises, aching muscles or the hunger grumbling softly in his belly.

He was on the hunt, and that was all that mattered. The rest of it could wait. He'd rest when it was finished, eat when there was time and bathe when he was sure that there was no more blood to spill.

This time, at least.

Because the hunt was never really over. Bolan's war was never done. There might be cease-fires, the occasional white flag of truce for mutual convenience, but he'd never sign a treaty with the predators who were his enemies. He couldn't fight them to a draw and walk away, believing that he'd managed to secure some short-term victory.

The war went on until he fell, or else became the last man standing on the battlefield. Right now, the battlefield was here, on Isla de Victoria. Tomorrow, if he lived, it would be somewhere else. New faces, varied motives, but the same old enemies.

War without end. Amen.

The jungle was his home, no matter what terrain surrounded him at any given moment. Bolan had long since accepted that and learned to live with it.

Someday, in turn, he'd die with it.

But maybe not this day.

THE DEAD MAN SPURRED them on. They picked up speed, gaining time, but without the reckless haste that warned every living thing within a mile that humans are tramping through the forest. Finding the corpse focused Johnny's attention, where it had begun to wander off in odd directions, dwelling on a future that would never be, the way a tongue returns over and over to the socket of a missing tooth.

They knew Tripp wasn't alone now. Mack had seen him leaving the camp with a small group of natives, and the dead man on the trail was proof he hadn't ditched them yet. The merc wouldn't have kept a wounded soldier with him for five minutes, much less two hours. Someone else had influenced Tripp, and those companions were leaving their mark on the forest, as well.

The signs were obvious. The soldiers trailing Garrett Tripp were city boys.

"We're close," Mack whispered at one point, coming up on three o'clock. Johnny was thirsty, but he didn't reach for his canteen. Instead, he concentrated on the trees around him, straining his senses for any trace of the enemy.

And fifteen minutes later, there he was.

Not Tripp, but a black man dressed in olive drab fatigues. They caught him pausing on the trail, some fifty feet ahead of them, and looking back the way he'd come. From the expression on his face, the soldier wasn't terribly surprised to find out he'd been followed. He had an M-16 and tried to use it, but Mack hit him with a short burst to the gut and dropped him where he stood.

Without waiting for orders, Johnny left the trail, right side, while Mack went to the left. The gut-shot rebel thrashed and wailed, but he was out of it for now. A mercy shot would only give the enemy a better fix on their position.

Johnny took his time, placing each step precisely, using his weapon to ease aside the tall grass and dangling vines. It seemed to take forever, but the creeping passage let him listen, first for sounds of hasty flight—there were none—then for any subtle noises of the enemy preparing his defense. Nothing.

He tried to put himself inside the mercenary's head. First thing, Tripp would be wondering about the gunfire. Since M-16 rifles all sounded alike, his first thought might be that his rear guard had triggered the shots. Just in case he was wrong, though, Tripp wouldn't call out to the guy and betray his position.

What would he do, instead?

Freeze, first. Then listen. If his native cohorts didn't give him the all-clear or tell him what was happening, the merc would have to find out for himself.

And there was no way he could do that standing still.

Johnny slowed his pace, feeling as if he'd stepped into the midst of a slow-motion film by mistake. It made him twitchy, ready to fire at the drop of a leaf, but now he had to think of Mack, as well as Tripp and an unknown number of rebel companions.

The way it happened, Johnny nearly missed the warning when it came, a shifting in the undergrowth beside him that was barely audible, the sort of noise a gentle breeze or creeping lizard might produce. Half turned in that direction, hesitating in midstride, he just had time to raise his carbine as a dark hand wrapped around a bright blade thrust out of the shadows, toward his face.

Johnny blocked it with microseconds to spare, steel grating on the carbine's plastic furniture. A rushing body bowled him over, crashing through a wall of ferns and something thorny that ripped his fatigues, finding flesh underneath. Damned thorns on everything, and now the carbine was crushing his chest, the enemy on top of him, while Johnny grappled for the knife. A moist, dark face loomed over him, teeth snapping at his throat.

The rebel wasn't big, but he was wiry and he fought with fierce determination, knowing that a loss at this stage of the game meant certain death. Johnny replied in kind, gouging and pummeling, using his knees, boots, elbows, any weapon he could to defend himself. The guns were useless with his hands full, but at least his adversary couldn't reach them, either.

As a sweat-slick wrist slipped through his fingers, Johnny felt the rebel fumbling at his holstered pistol. Snarling, Johnny reared up for a head butt to the other's face and was rewarded with a dull crack and a splash of blood onto his cheeks.

His knee found something soft and evidently painful, grinding as he shifted, and he put his weight behind it. His enemy began to squeal. Johnny increased the pressure, at the same time striking with a forearm to his adversary's throat. It wasn't hard enough to kill—he lacked the leverage for that— but it produced a wheezing cry.

The shiny blade came slashing at his face again, but Johnny blocked it, turned the wrist and forced it toward his adversary's throat. The other man was trembling, fighting back with every ounce of his remaining power.

"Die, already!" Johnny whispered to him through clenched teeth. "Just fucking die!"

THE BURST OF GUNFIRE from behind him made Tripp duck into the clingy undergrowth, then freeze. He waited for one of his soldiers to give the all-clear, ruefully explain that he'd killed a snake or was firing at shadows, but neither of them spoke. He waited for another moment, poised to fight or flee, then heard a crashing, ponderous commotion in the forest to his left.

Tripp couldn't see a thing from where he was, but he could judge the situation fairly well by sound alone. The thrashing noise he heard was not an animal in flight, because it didn't fade away. Also, the nature of the sounds told him the body— make that bodies—tumbling through the brush were bigger than the island's largest animals.

It had to be men fighting, then, and one of them was his.

Where was the other one?

Tripp had a feeling that he'd seen the last of that one, whichever had taken the hits. From his experience, if either of his men could reach their weapons, they'd be lighting up the forest now, full-auto fire deployed without a thought for targets, Tripp, or personal security. It should have sounded like

Times Square on New Year's Eve, but all he heard were those infernal grappling, grunting sounds.

Instead of moving toward the noise and trying to assist his man, Tripp circled slowly, cautiously, away to his right. The best-case scenario, from his point of view, was a single pursuer who shot one of his men, then stumbled into hands-on combat with the other. If that was the case, Tripp could leave them to kill one another and flee like a thief in the night.

He pictured the captive who had turned the tables, humiliating Tripp and nearly killing him one short day earlier. That man would have the guts to double back and raid the camp, all right, but could he pull it off alone? Could he fling two grenades that far apart in the early moments of the firefight? And where would he get hand grenades?

A rifle, Tripp could figure. Kill a sentry, take his gun and you were good to go. But guards at his camp weren't issued hand grenades.

So, figure more than one pursuer. That meant Tripp could not afford to turn his back a second time. The slick bastards had nearly tagged him as he was leaving the camp. They'd killed one of his men in the process and wounded another— the lame duck who had slowed Tripp down and let the hunters overtake him, damn it.

Stop them here, he thought. Once and for all.

But thinking it was one thing; doing it was something else. Tripp didn't know how many adversaries he was facing, much less where they were or how well armed.

A sudden silence in the forest froze Tripp with his left foot raised to take another step. The brawl was evidently settled, one way or the other, but he had no way of finding out who'd won. Maybe the two had killed each other, which would thin the opposition ranks at least, but Tripp couldn't be sure.

He waited, blinking salty sweat out of his eyes, but not before it stung him. Tripp could wipe his face, but that meant taking one hand off his rifle, and possibly revealing his position.

Fuck it. Let it sting.

The problem was, it blurred his vision, too. He imagined that the shadows twenty feet in front of him were moving, taking shape. It was a man's shape, he decided—or perhaps it was a stationary shrub, a simple trick of light.

Breathing shallowly, between clenched teeth, Tripp shivered from the tension, aching for release. He couldn't let the enemy get any closer, if it was an enemy, and not a frigging optical illusion.

There! It moved again!

Or did it?

Fairly sobbing with frustration, Tripp tightened his finger and unleashed a blazing stream of automatic fire.

BOLAN WAS NEVER SURE what saved him. Something shifted in the shadows up ahead, and he was diving for the cover of a hulking tree as gunfire blazed in front of him, a stream of bullets shredding ferns and creepers, chipping bark. He took advantage of the noise and wriggled to the far side of the tree, risking a glance around its bulk.

Another muzzle-flash blazed in the forest's murk, sweeping across the point where Bolan had been standing seconds earlier. He heard the bullets hissing, snapping, whining, but they weren't for him. The forest swallowed them and passed them on.

He marked the muzzle-flare and fired a short burst of his own, not really banking on a hit, but hoping for the best. At once, the hostile weapon swung around to bring him under fire, raking the tree that sheltered Bolan, chewing up the turf mere inches from his knees.

Too close for comfort, that was, but he'd lived through worse.

It was impossible to count the rounds on autofire, but Bolan knew that unmodified M-16s devoured ammo at a cyclic rate somewhere between 700 and 950 rounds per minute. Unless the sniper had some kind of custom magazine, he ought to be reloading now, and that gave Bolan time to try another angle of attack.

He released the pin of the last grenade Johnny had given him and sent it looping toward his adversary with a sidearm pitch. Six seconds on the fuse, and he was counting down the numbers as his enemy unleashed another spray of fire.

The blast was muffled slightly by the brooding forest, but its shock wave still reached out for Bolan where he crouched, behind the giant tree. He waited for the shards of shrapnel to exhaust their deadly force, then broke from cover, sprinting along a diagonal course to a point on the shooter's left flank.

It was a gamble. His enemy might have survived the blast unscathed, or Bolan might run into someone else, all primed and ready for a killing shot. It didn't happen, though, and he slid into cover after closing half the distance to his enemy's last-known position.

"You bastards!" Even with its unfamiliar ragged edge, he recognized Tripp's voice. "You want me, come ahead. What are you waiting for?"

Beneath the rasp, there was a weakness to the voice that Bolan hadn't heard before. Was Tripp wounded? Or was this the award-winning performance that he hoped would save his life?

"Just do me one favor," Tripp called from the shadows. "Before we finish this, for Christ's sake tell me who you are!"

The Executioner took a chance.

"You wouldn't know me," Bolan answered, though in fact Tripp likely would have recognized his name.

Instead of probing fire, the weary voice came back at Bolan. "Right. Okay. Try this one, then—who sent you after me?"

Bolan was moving as he spoke. "Someone who doesn't want a country owned by criminals this close to home."

"Well, shit, that narrows down the field." Tripp laughed. "Show me a government that isn't run by criminals, and I'll be on the next plane out."

"Too late for that," Bolan said, moving.

"Right. I guess you're here to punch my ticket, eh?"

"I want the men who hired you," Bolan told him honestly.

"You're welcome to 'em. Happy hunting." There was bitterness behind the pain that time.

"If you feel that way," Bolan said, edging closer, "why not tell me where to find them?"

"I'd be glad to," Tripp replied from hiding, "but I'm not exactly on their A-list at the moment, if you catch my drift. In fact, the fuckers want me dead as much as you do."

Want to bet? Bolan thought. But he said, "No ties to cut, then. Why not give them up?"

"Does that get me a pass?"

"Why not?" Bolan had no qualms about lying to a murderer.

Tripp paused a moment, maybe thinking, maybe gathering his strength. Bolan could hear him shifting in the undergrowth. It sounded clumsy, but he wasn't sure what should be made of that.

"Okay," Tripp said at last. "There's one place they might go that you people haven't busted yet. No promises, you understand. I definitely won't be getting any invitations to the next sit-down."

You got that right, the warrior told himself. And said, "Where's that?"

"In Mexico. You ever been to Acapulco?"

"Once or twice," Bolan replied.

"There's a hotel. The International. Somebody owns a piece of it. I'm pretty sure it's Santiago. They fly in a couple times a year and shoot the shit. No promises, but that's the place I'd watch if I were waiting for the gang to rendezvous."

"I'll make a note," Bolan said. Almost there.

"So, I can split?"

"Not quite."

The barking laugh again. "You bastards. All the same." He paused, then added, "Hell, I wouldn't let you walk out, either. Where's the fun in that?"

"I'm not in this for fun," Bolan said.

"You need to relax, my friend. It's all a game, you know?" The voice was drawing nearer, with a scuffling noise behind it. "It's a game, but somebody keeps changing all the rules."

Tripp broke through the trees with a lurching stride, his fatigues smeared with crimson, firing from the hip with a muddy M-16. Bolan lined up his shot and squeezed off, aware in that instant of another rifle firing from his left, toward Tripp.

The merc absorbed a dozen hits, two dozen, and went down firing, rifle pinned beneath him as his death grip emptied out the magazine. There was no need to check him for a pulse.

Johnny emerged from cover, moving cautiously to Bolan's side.

"Feel any better?" Bolan asked.

"Not yet."

"Okay. I've got a little something that may help."

14

Acapulco, Mexico

A limousine was waiting at the airport. Maxwell Reed and Merrill Harris let a porter wheel their baggage on his cart and load it in the limo's spacious trunk. Their driver tipped the porter, freeing Reed to concentrate on more important things.

He wasn't fond of Mexico. The water didn't bother him—a lifetime in the tropics had accustomed Reed to most bacteria and parasites—but he disliked the dry heat and the country's work ethic, or lack of one. Reed counted laziness among the mortal sins, and he would never understand a culture that revolved around siestas. On the other hand, when he considered the corruption that was rife in Mexico, it almost made him feel at home.

The Hotel International rated five stars in most guidebooks. This visit marked the fourth time Reed had stayed there, as a guest of Hector Santiago and the others. In the past they'd met to speak of strategy and future plans. This time, Reed and his sponsors would discuss whether his dream might still come true, or whether he'd be cast aside.

"How did it come to this?" he asked.

Harris leaned forward in his seat. "Sir, if I may—"

"It was rhetorical," Reed said. "No answer is expected or required."

"No, sir. But if I may…"

"Go on, then." If you must.

"I think there's room for optimism, yet," Harris declared.

"Oh, really?"

"Yes, sir! Think of all your sponsors who have invested in this cause. They're pragmatists, if nothing else. They recognize a winning cause, and they will not be eager to abandon their investment."

"Winners *win*, Merrill. Can you recall the last time we achieved a victory? Remind me, if you can, because it's slipped my mind."

"I grant you, sir, the past few weeks have been a disappointing time."

"You have a gift for understatement, Merrill."

"But the polls from home still indicate a solid margin of support for change. Halsey still has the handicaps he started with—his arrogance, corruption, public ties to Washington and London."

"But he has the army's loyalty. They beat us every time we take the field. As for the other business, without Tripp…"

Reed let it go. He didn't care to think about the many negatives just now. No doubt he'd be reminded of them in detail by his assembled sponsors in a few short hours.

"But if the sponsors still desire the same result, sir, who else is there for them to support?"

"We'll soon find out," Reed muttered. "Now be quiet, Merrill, and let me think in peace."

They finished off the silent ride and passed into the lobby of the International, with bellhops and their luggage bringing up

the rear. The oily manager was waiting for them, bowing from
the waist as he greeted Reed, escorting them to the elevator.

"You have the presidential suite, *señor.* It's only fitting, yes?"

Reed didn't know if it was fitting or a hollow mockery, but
he responded as a statesman should. "Thank you. Please give
the staff my greeting, and express my gratitude."

The manager was beaming now. "You are too kind, *señor.*
Too generous. We're honored by your presence. Any friend
of Señor Santiago's—"

Reed supposed it was his scowl that made the manager fall
silent for the short duration of their elevator ride.

SEMYON BORODIN SIPPED nicely chilled vodka and thought
about what he would say when they were all assembled to as-
sess the damage they had suffered. He'd rehearsed the speech
in private a dozen times, making changes here and there, fine-
tuning it, and still he looked for ways to make it better.

Ways to let the others know who was in charge.

He couldn't say it right out loud, that way, of course. Although he'd brought security along, so had the others, and
he'd never make it out of the hotel alive. The International was
Santiago's roost, after all, and there was certain protocol to
be observed.

Still, Borodin was optimistic. He believed the Sicilians
would support him. They were all Europeans, of a sort, and
distrusted Third World types as a matter of course. They'd
seen the ruin brought about by Sun and Santiago, with their
pigheaded refusals to get rid of Garrett Tripp.

At least the mercenary was no longer with them. Someone
else had seen to that. And while the mysterious strangers had
Borodin's thanks for that, they still posed a threat to the cartel. There had been talk of giving up the plan entirely, leav-

ing Reed to twist in the wind, but Borodin had argued for tenacity.

He'd won that argument, at least, but whether he could win the next and most important one was anybody's guess. Even with the Sicilians backing him, he'd have to sway one of the others for the vote to go his way. Tanaka was a possibility, if Borodin could work the natural distrust between the triads and the Yakuza to his advantage.

Borodin drained his glass and said "More vodka" to no one in particular. The nearest of his bodyguards rushed to fill the order, while Borodin fired a cheroot with his solid-gold lighter. His glass came back cold and brimming with crystal-clear liquor.

It would be his last drink before the meeting, Borodin promised himself. He wouldn't get tipsy on three or four vodkas, but the sit-down was too critical for him to take silly risks. The others would be on alert, troubled by recent losses, itching for a fight if they perceived some underhanded move in progress.

And the last thing Borodin needed—the last thing he'd be able to survive—was a war fought on four fronts at once.

Diplomacy, he thought. A game for fools.

But he could play it with the best of them when necessary. Like today.

His diamond-studded watch showed Borodin he had another hour to wait before his so-called comrades gathered to debate their next move. It wasn't long, but patience was a virtue Borodin had never cultivated. Delayed gratification had never been his strong point.

But if the others could wait, so could he.

His glass was empty, and Borodin couldn't remember draining it. That was bad, a sign of alcoholism according to most of the books, but Borodin dismissed it as a side effect of his distraction and impatience. Anyway, it was his last drink of the day, at least until after the meeting.

Had he enjoyed it?

Borodin couldn't remember, but the vodka plainly had not relaxed him. His nerves were still taut, his mind still churning overtime, editing and amending his speech.

If they turned against him, Borodin would be in danger. Bearing that in mind, he'd made arrangements for specific tools to be delivered, ready for retrieval when his entourage left the airport. A brief detour, two extra suitcases added to their stock of luggage, and Borodin felt that his men were ready for anything.

At least, as ready as they could be.

The trick, he understood, would be to strike the proper tone: persuasive, but not threatening, the proper blend of emotion and logic.

Frowning, Borodin recalled the words of his mentor, long dead now. "Sincerity is the key. If you can fake that, you'll go far."

Borodin missed the irony but got the message.

Still, his nerves...

"More vodka!" he demanded, holding out the empty glass.

THE CONFERENCE ROOM was almost ready. Hector Santiago moved around the table, making minuscule adjustments to the chairs, the water pitchers, glasses, ashtrays. Unlike other business gatherings the Hotel International had hosted in the past, there were no pens or notepads on the table. There were no projectors, screens, laptops, or colorful brochures.

The corporation that was meeting here today kept no minutes, put nothing on paper, saved nothing on disks or hard drives. None who gathered in that room were strangers to the subject. They required no memos or reports to bring them up to speed.

Twelve minutes by his watch, and Santiago felt the tension as the first of his invited guests arrived. There was no outward display of tension among them, but Santiago had his ear to the ground and knew when discontent was brewing. More specifically, the Colombian thought he knew who was responsible.

Santiago counted heads as the delegates filed in and took their seats, each man accompanied by a trusted aide-de-camp. Semyon Borodin wore a self-satisfied look on his face, while Sun Zu-wang displayed his usual reserve. Kenji Tanaka and Tomichi Kano, present for the Yakuza, smiled blandly at the room but greeted none of their colleagues specifically. The two Sicilians, Ambrosio and Calabria, rarely joined these gatherings except by telephone, but this time they'd bestirred themselves to make a personal appearance. Maxwell Reed and his aide arrived last, stylishly late, and received abbreviated greetings from each of the others in turn.

When all were present, Santiago urged them to sample the buffet and liquor. They had vital business to discuss, but Santiago wanted them relaxed, if possible. Food and drink might take the edge off and prevent a flare-up during the proceedings. With any luck, the Colombian thought, he might be able to defuse a deadly situation before it exploded.

And if not, well, perhaps he could channel the blast to his own advantage. Maybe profit by the situation after all.

Diplomacy was the domain of cheats and liars.

Santiago loved it.

He filled a plate, poured whiskey for himself, then took his seat at the head of the table. The cartel had no leader per se, but the host of any particular gathering served as chairman in acknowledgment of his effort and expense. Whatever slim advantage it provided, Santiago worried that antipathy between the others might undo his efforts to negotiate a truce.

But there was also profit to be made in war.

He watched the others eating, noted that several leaders spoke primarily to their own lieutenants when they spoke at all. Borodin had barely touched his food before he turned to Santiago, asking, "Has this room been swept for listening devices?"

Santiago nodded amiably. "Yes, indeed. Technicians scanned the room—the whole floor, in fact—at eight o'clock this morning."

"Five hours ago?" The Russian frowned. "Has anyone had access to the room since then?"

"Myself, of course," Santiago replied. "And hotel personnel."

"Before we get down to business," Borodin said, "I assume you won't object to sweeping it again? Just to be on the safe side, of course." The Russian's smile spoke volumes of contempt for Santiago's security arrangements.

"Of course not," he replied. A soldier stooped beside him and received the whispered order. To the delegates, he said, "It will take some time to scan the room again, my friends. I trust you'll all enjoy yourselves while we put Semyon's mind at ease."

"THIS STRIKES ME as a waste of time," Sun Zu-wang said.

"You won't think so if they turn up a microphone," Borodin replied.

Sun regarded the Russian with thinly veiled contempt. "I trust our host," he said. "There is no reason to believe his preparations have been careless."

"Nor have I suggested it," the Russian said, bristling. "All

I say is that we've had too many difficulties in the past few weeks. We've lost too many men, too much material and money. Someone knows each move before we make it. If there is a leak somewhere, we all deserve to know it."

"Now you have insulted Mr. Santiago," Sun observed.

"I haven't! He had no objection to another sweep."

Sun interrupted the Colombian. "I can't help thinking Mr. Borodin would be gravely insulted if any such lapse of security was suggested at a meeting under his sponsorship."

"Nonsense!" the Russian snapped. "There'd be no need for it, of course, but I take no offense at a constructive criticism."

Sun's narrow smile encompassed all present. "May we assume, Comrade Borodin, that your definition of constructive criticism is limited to helpful advice?"

"I always try to help," Borodin said. His aide was stone-faced, giving Sun the evil eye.

"And that would not include false accusations of conspiracy against your allies in the present venture, I suppose?" Sun asked.

"Conspiracy? This is a term for lawyers and policemen," Borodin replied. "Say what you mean."

"We are surrounded every day by rumors," Sun continued. "Some are harmless, others are pernicious. Some are launched deliberately, with the intent to harm. If I suggested, for example, that some person at this table hoped to sow dissent among the others for his own profit, you would be right to question me, demand his name and ask for proof."

"I've heard no accusations of that sort," Santiago interjected. "Perhaps—"

"Perhaps not," Sun pressed on, "but someone, I believe, would gladly see our coalition shattered, all our effort wasted."

"Why should this come as a surprise to anyone? We've been under attack for two weeks now. An enemy has tracked our every movement. None of us is safe!" Borodin was shouting.

Sun paused as the door opened to admit one of Santiago's technicians. The man carried a device resembling a portable radio, which had a plastic wand attached to it by cable. Silent and intent, the newcomer began to circle the room slowly, passing his wand over the walls, the furniture, anything that stood in his path. His sensor emitted no sound but a quiet hiss of static.

"Perhaps," Sun continued, "we've spent too much time looking outside our own circle for the enemy. Perhaps that foe has been among us, all along."

Beet-red above his collar, Borodin shot back, "I also have considered this and find it plausible. What better mask for treachery than friendship's smile?"

Hector Santiago rapped the table with his knuckles. "Gentlemen, I must insist that you—"

A low warbling sound interrupted the Colombian's speech. All eyes swung toward the technician, who in turn was eyeing his machine.

"What is it?" Santiago asked.

"I'm not sure, sir. Something…curious."

That said, the young man made his way around the room, watching the others watching him, wielding his wand as the sound from his receiver rose in pitch, its ululations becoming more rapid.

"You see!" Borodin blurted out. "As I thought!"

"Is it a bug?" Santiago asked.

"No, sir. Microphones produce a whine. This sound is…different."

Borodin muttered something unintelligible, turning in his

seat to watch the young man work. Sun tracked the stranger as he came to the buffet, passing his slender wand above the platters of food. From his receiver, the warbling sound was now more rapid, almost trilling. By the time he reached the mobile bar, Sun's ears could hardly separate the rapid pulses of the sound.

"It's here," the technician said, "somewhere."

First, he scanned the bottles, then the unused glasses and the ice dispenser. Finally, he knelt to open the cabinet beneath the bar itself, where Sun presumed more liquor bottles would be stored. He heard the young man gasp.

"What is it?" Santiago demanded.

"Get out! It's a—"

BOLAN WAITED for the blast, and when it came, the gushing fireball was reflected in the lenses of his sunglasses. The conference room's windows blew outward, smoke and flame erupting as if hell had vented through a portion of the Hotel International.

Maybe it had.

Beside him, Johnny held the remote-control detonator in his hand. One end of a hotel waiter's clip-on bow tie protruded from the pocket of his cheap white shirt. Black slacks and shoes completed the generic uniform.

Two days of surveillance and electronic eavesdropping had preceded the hit. With Stony Man's assistance, they had charted the movements of various cartel VIPs, tracking them en route to Acapulco and Santiago's hotel. The rest of it had been relatively simple, though not without risk.

Johnny had done the hardest part, insisting that the inside job was his alone. It had required some finesse, but the kid was never short in that department. They had built the bomb

together and Johnny had carried it in, bagged a uniform on
the sly, done the rest on sheer nerve and raw fury.

Now it was done, with alarms clamoring and sirens wailing in the distance. An explosion and fire at a five-star hotel
brought out Acapulco's finest in force.

Too late.

The brothers lingered long enough to watch the first fire
trucks arrive, then walked back to the rental car they'd parked
a block away from the hotel. Along the way, Johnny wiped the
detonator clean of fingerprints and pitched it into a storm drain.

At the car, they turned once more and stared at the hotel.
Black smoke rising against the sky.

"Do you feel better now?" Bolan asked.

Johnny was unreadable behind his shades.

"I'm getting there," he said.

Stony Man is deployed against an armed
invasion on American soil...

COLD
OBJECTIVE

A Seattle-based oil tycoon has put his wealth and twisted
vision to work in a quest to control the world's oil reserves.
He's got what it takes to pull it off: the Russian mafiya on his
payroll, and Middle East sympathizers willing to die to see
America burn. And if that's not enough, he's got the nukes
and bioweapons to bring the world to its knees. Stony Man
unleashes an all-out assault, knowing that a few good men
are all it takes to stand up, be counted and face down evil.
Or die trying.

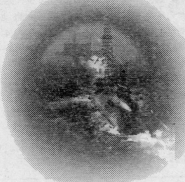

STONY
MAN ®

*Available
October 2004
at your favorite
retail outlet.*

TAKE 'EM FREE

2 action-packed novels plus a mystery bonus

NO RISK
NO OBLIGATION TO BUY